SEARCHERS AT THE GULF

Franklin Russell

SEARCHERS

AT THE GULF

W · W · Norton & Company · Inc ·

New York

For the young Jackie

Much is known about the Gulf, but most of it is mysterious. It is too complex, too contradictory, to be frozen in fact; only fiction gives some sense of its life.

The Gulf described here is not real. The author has not tried to write with scientific precision about an actual place. But if the fictional Gulf resembles any place, it is the Gulf of St. Lawrence, on North America's eastern coast. The real Gulf mixes north and south, provides a meeting place for whale and seal, seabird and landbird, barren and forest, an extraordinary confluence of life from the microcosmic to the giant. It has survived man's occupation with much of its primeval atmosphere intact.

The Gulf of St. Lawrence resembles the fictional Gulf. It has as many creatures and plants as the fictional Gulf, or perhaps more. For every creature described in the fiction, the real Gulf has a thousand such characters.

Either Gulf may yield whatever a searcher chooses to find in it.

—F.R.

SEARCHERS AT THE GULF

Chapter ONE

I

The Gulf was shaped like an eye and set on earth between arctic and equator. It felt the antagonisms of both extremes and breathed with hybrid passion. Every life within its broad salt waters was charged with this tension of extremes and so the Gulf was a place of compromise. It resisted equally the fanatic ice and the permeating heat. Its lack of allegiance to north or south or hot or cold made it the most diverse place on earth.

An autocrat, the Gulf ruled the flow of eggs and the stocks of food; its decisions demanded obedience from billions of lives inside it and so created a universal order. It was at once dictator and a stage for the dictatorial process, and on its many-leveled platform countless dramas of creation and destruction were acted out with millions of daily revisions. Minuscule on this spacious stage, the players moved unerringly, like puppets, their blind discipline mocking freedom. Or so it seemed.

Every creature felt the pressure of the Gulf as it pushed each one to the limits of territory and of survival. The creatures responded—mortal, fallible, but never resigned. They went down with limbs and claws and fins and wings outstretched in protest. The natural end was death, and the Gulf apportioned death impartially. They struggled, and the force of the fight bent the path of death, turned it left and right, and fashioned it into ironic circles. The ingenuity of their struggle often delayed the moment of the end, and thus obedience was sometimes modified by the will to survive.

The elliptic Gulf was closed in by four shores, each individual because of soil or rock or river or forest. The bleak northern shore, rockbound and thinly forested, ran a hundred rocky valleys south into the Gulf, and each bore a short, tumbling river refugee from nearby rock mountains. The western shore, black-soiled, thick-treed, ran long calm rivers east into the Gulf through deep and ancient woods. The south shore, red-soiled, gardenlike, evoked tropical memories with flowers and fruits and forests gladed across rich plains, its shore a rolling strand of yellow beaches. East, where the Gulf should have opened its mouth into the ocean, a big island bulked across it.

14

Granite-bodied, thin-soiled, mountainous, it pressed so close against the northern and southern shores that the water exits were compressed into two narrow straits. The Gulf received refreshing stimulus from the earth's other seas and flowed away its effluent water through them.

The Gulf was studded with hundreds of smaller islands, some small enough to be crowded by a score of pines, others big enough to house a million nesting seabirds. They clustered unevenly along the western shore and were strung along the northern shore like a rocky necklace. The Gulf was both deep and shallow, riven by submarine valleys and demarked by underwater meadowlands where fish hordes grazed. Throughout, its creatures ran obedient to its complex geography.

The herring massed on submarine ledges in the western Gulf, fifty feet underwater, and laid billions of eggs in seven days during on autumnal equinox. This was their duty, repeated twenty thousand years in this place. A school of herring surfaced one brilliant midspring morning and the Gulf's bright face darkened with ripples across fifty square miles. Another dark patch moved inward. The two herring nations collided, folded into each other, and parted, still intact, still submissive to their separate ages and purposes.

The flounder, flat and sand-hugging, with eyes migrant in their skulls, hunted at strictly designated depths; some were held at fifty feet, others at two hundred. They could not join other species of their family at five hundred feet, nor did they have need to, and they would never

15

know those aristocrats of the family who lived in pitch-black depths a half mile down.

Cod armadas filled the Gulf in every season and gamboled at its surface, then abruptly went to one thousand feet and spread wide across the bottom. Cod waited in dim greenish haze for Gulf signals of spring, and then swarmed upward from submarine valleys and prairies to rampageous assignations with victims directed to the slaughter by the dictatorial Gulf.

The roles were made perfect by generations of practice. Geese touched Gulf skies with high, remote barking, the first of a procession of spring players. Ducks, fleet as clots of mist, robins and blackbirds and bluebirds rushed north, each arrival obeying his schedule, the meadowlarks running ahead of the purple finches, the vireos bunched together with groups of warblers. After summering in the highlands of the big island, the caribou came streaming down and headed for the one small lowland sheltered place where they knew they could survive the winter. In the spring new shoots of balsam fir sprouted obediently to fuel them back to the highlands.

Seals rode rocking ice pans into the Gulf and whelped in blizzards, obedient to dates set in and by the Gulf a year before. Mackerel jammed the Gulf from another direction, as strictly controlled as the rushing birds. They convulsed the sea for a moment, swept the surface clear that day, then dashed on in ravenous haste.

At a signal, birds poured out of the sea and colonized cliffs on all shores, islands everywhere, and estuaries along the western shore. Birds came by land, showing bright colors and odd forms to the Gulf. They did not hesitate until they had occupied every valley, every beach, every river, tree, mountain, lake, and pond in all the Gulf territory.

Halibut eggs, laid in the darkest deeps, rose until exactly one thousand feet of water lay above them, and hovered there while their enemies hunted them above and below. The salmon, disciplined into separate armies, with coats as dark as night from their long sea journey halfway around the hemisphere, paused at the mouths of rivers on every shore and then rushed inland in passionate waves of attack to find one place each, gravel bottoms to dig and lay down eggs, such places incomprehensibly remembered.

Squid appeared out of abyssal waters, their origins enigmatic but their youth undeniable, and their movement into the Gulf was headlong. These first-year creatures knew their time and place with utter precision; they knew exactly where they must go, though they had never been there; they knew exactly what they must do, though they had never done it before. With them rode relentless pilot whales who pursued the squid, their only food. Interdependence was the touchstone; each life in the Gulf hinged delicately on another, and the absence or malfunction of the one killed or deformed the other.

17

II

The eye of the Gulf was closed now in winter sleep. Many of its creatures, stationed far apart in this time of ice, awaited their moment, soon upon them, to act out a new season. In a forest on the Gulf's big island, a lynx wrinkled his nose and scanned a dusky frozen inlet, sensitive to its occasional offer of a victim. He slid through the trees and his wide-booted paw pads imprinted the snow but did not sink into it. He was a Gulf animal, and wore down the winter in ceaseless pursuit of the elusive hare, a white-coated wraith who danced an invitation among the trees. There he was! The lynx darted forward. But there was no hare.

He hunted the phantom hare with sullen, catlike determination, forty pounds of lean and anguished muscle behind expressionless eyes. His whiskers and furry jowls drooped and his black-tipped bobtail jerked in the cold. The ice mirrored a floating, fantastic image of his intent face, and then cracked into a thousand faces.

A white eagle hung motionless from the center of the sky; this morning he seemed cut from marble. His shadow came down across the northern shore and wandered among stray seals, then slid, oily as blubber, into the water. He hauled himself up very high and hard against the wind, blinking ice crystals from his eyes, and swept the shore for longspurs and buntings and ptarmigans and frozen fish, but he saw nothing. He left the shore and hung himself above the top of a high mountain a hundred miles away, and stayed there, remote and silent and accusatory of the Gulf which had frustrated his strongest urge.

The codfish massed in dark conglomerations, awaiting the moment they would dance odd and irreverent jigs to the tunes of the Gulf. They faced into scarce-felt currents, fins gesturing, each group a common size, the smallest fish clustering on the center of a mid-Gulf plateau and lining the shores of northern shore islands, the larger fish waiting out the winter in deeper, darker places. One of them a giant, a quarter of a century old, two hundred pounds of flesh and bone, had expanded into the Gulf, *his* Gulf, and began each new year bigger than the last. His size and appetite forever separated him from his fellow cod. While they swam in their comradely age groups, graduated precisely in size, he wandered a lonely journey in perpetual search for enough, always enough. But the more he ate, the more he grew. He was never satisfied. He ate small cod and crabs and shrimp and shellfish—anything—and his voracious maw put him nowhere and everywhere at once. He consumed himself, as it were, to survive. He was a giant, omnivorous, a wanderer perforce, hungry by tradition, and now at the edge of an ambiguous season in his deepest waters.

At the bottom of the southern Gulf a fortress squatted, unmoving, periscope eyes aglisten, armored tail folded under, great claws at rest. The lobster was the most inert of all Gulf creatures. He had retired behind armor rather than fly or swim or run fleet across the snow. He was neither aggressive nor bold, but his passivity was ingenious. His brain was tiny, and his blue blood flowed reluctantly through narrow veins. He did not migrate anywhere, and although he could walk like a steel-sheathed ballet dancer on the tips of his eight spindly legs, he fled backward, and badly, so that flight often ended in collision rather than refuge. He was prized by too many of the other sea creatures. They knew how to reach him. In periodic crises his fortress walls fell to ridiculous rubble and left him naked and timorous. His armor, for all its strength, was an impediment to his personality. Behind it he could watch coldly while less well-prepared creatures, the shellfish, the ultimate fortresses, had their shells chipped away by crabs. He watched while one swift crab claw was thrust inside the broken shell and a soft clam body was twirled aloft and carried away. He watched other creatures fight and sensed the flailing of a swordfish's tail on the sea above. Then he moved cautiously from his refuge to feed on the sinking detritus of the great fish's victims. The lobster chanced nothing, contributed nothing except his sense of caution. He was a prisoner in his fortress and his mind was small behind the walls so that he was forever unable to reach higher; his search for security had killed adventure.

A robin stood in the summit of a leaning cedar, surrounded by a light dusting of frost, and looked north. His big, bright, humorous eyes twinkled in the sun and his russet chest fluffed fat. He was a Gulf creature, born in a valley on its western shore, although a thousand miles from it now. He had made the fall migration and return and had bred six youngsters in two nests. Now, for his second flight north, he was wagering against high odds; his time was long past. He had survived beyond eighteen months, and this was an indulgence for a mere singer, a troubadour of the forest. His life had been made meaningless by the survival of his progeny. The Gulf did not need more robins of his kind, and he would live there under sufferance. He fluted a short ode to the coming northern flight and struck a robin's pose against a network of bare beech tips.

Another Gulf creature, as far removed as the robin, waited out his winter time to the east and north, in a place even more cold-bitten than the Gulf. This was the grilse, a young salmon, a handsome, eager virgin whose winter was a boring wait before the race for home in the waters of a modest Gulf river. He lived now in a commonwealth of salmon which had collected in a broad submarine valley where the nearby shore debouched glacial ice. This was a polyglot nation of aliens drawn from a hundred shores spread all over the hemisphere, and when the call came to move they would scatter. Millions of them came from the Gulf, more millions from the eastern hemisphere. They mingled, fraternal for the moment, while ice sank deep limbs among them.

The grilse must seek one river, finding it after an east-west expedition that took him accurately against storm-created currents and the southern flow of the hemisphere waters. He must aim himself to avoid seals and killer whales, rest in the lea of islands, navigate the territory of the codfish until, finally, he must ascend a river which would attempt to push him back into the Gulf. There he would be in the territory of the robin.

A secretive Gulf creature, the petrel was a bird of the storm, a gray speck in the oceans. Three thousand miles from the Gulf at this moment, she stood on the tip of a wave and danced a solemn jig. She could literally walk on water, and shared this talent with no other sea animal. She was the greatest wanderer of all. She would go part way around the earth to carry out one tiny assignment in the Gulf. She would be ecstatic over the running grilse, and her penetrating night cries might rouse the eagle as she sped through the night. She might move quickly under the nose of the lynx and dance just beyond the reaching lips of the cod. She would not meet the robin or know the lobster in her small, specialist place in the Gulf: a hole three inches wide on an insignificant western shore island. Pointed wings supplicating, she would dance, and wait, and then suddenly compress the essence of the sea into one creative act.

No hint of this was suggested now. The coast against which she flew sweated with tropical heat; the ocean was thick and stupid with it. Weeds floated under her. She was alone. She flew along the trough of a long wave, past an island projecting vertical black spires, and so moved on south in equatorial waters, away from the Gulf.

III

Soon animals would animate the Gulf. Their personalities would meld with the many moods of the Gulf earth. But now the eagle soared alone in air made brittle by his passage through it and, underneath, the great island turned, white and remote in the grip of this dead season. It stretched beyond the eagle's range of vision to the east, sitting on a base of granite dropped where the mouth of the Gulf should have opened freely to the sea. It was a dour island, able to express itself only in strength. The eagle drifted north along its western shore, oblivious to its gray coasts straining to stop the Gulf from bursting out into the open sea but knowing of its grudging release of Gulf waters through two narrow straits at its north and south ends.

White-capped and passive under the winter sun, the island seemed to deny that it was world headquarters for many sea creatures who found there a place to time themselves against the heartbeat of the solid earth. The island drew herring to its shores and lured capelin to smother its beaches with eggs. It invited migrant salmon and rapid

23

char and seduced colony upon colony of screaming gulls to line its southern cliffs. The island was host to the gannets, who commanded inaccessible cliffs and settled in their graceful, negligent way in white bazaars. The island called in the kittiwakes, dainty northern waifs, and gave them cliffs and offshore islands too steep for other birds, and there they fastened tiny nests to tiny ledges.

The island was an invitation for murres, black-suited and saturnine, and they covered low offshore scraps of granite with black masses of squirming life whose density and uproar repelled all who saw them. The island was a magnet for humorless puffins and gave them offshore headquarters with soil enough to excavate cities underground.

The island would waken, as would the Gulf, and draw its creatures in a season of splendid plenty. Pilot whales, driven mad by the proximity of too much food, would dash themselves to death against its shores, and the frantic squid, heedless in chase of helpless prey, would charge the island's beaches, vaned bodies stranding before they understood such folly.

The island's pointed northern end bisected an arctic current, a drift, and split its energy equally, sending one half into the Gulf, directing the other down the island's eastern shore. The drift brought down stuff flushed from tundra and glacial valley; it was a messenger from a thousand arctic places, a plankton bearer, a replenisher of the Gulf. In almost all seasons it spawned a continuing chain reaction of life wherever it touched.

The eagle paused over the drift and watched it compress its bulk through the northern strait, and he saw ice wedged on top of itself, heard the mutter and squeal of its compression. He looked for seals, who often choked the strait by the million as they came into the Gulf, but there was no sign of them yet.

The southern strait was known to him also, but it was far to the south, and not frozen. It was a highway for refugees in flight from the seasons or from their enemies, a brief territory for wandering cod, a route for urgent salmon and wary seabirds, a barrier for migrants across the land, a congregation point for hunters harrying the travelers, a place for killer whales and thrasher sharks, for dogfish and tuna and the fish with swords.

The moods of the Gulf were many, created by soil and rock as well as by more elemental forces. The eagle drifted on, crossing the northern strait, and moved along the Gulf's gray northern shore where a thin mantle of earth on a shield of crystalline rock offered the challenging proposition that life was possible there. The challenge was taken up by bleak low hills running inland, dressed in spruce and birch and pine, and by creeping shrubs and modest, crouching grasses showing along hundreds of miles of rocky teeth. The eagle faded into pallid, frozen haze and was lost in the north.

The western shore of the Gulf expanded into snow-lined rolling forest hills which marched south in a land clearly more life-receptive than the northern shore. Echoes of songbirds clung to leaning trees; this shore attracted music, pulling simple melodies from illusive southern refuges and bringing them to passionate, unexpected northern climaxes.

The western shore, with its inlets, estuaries, and bright streams dashing into slow rivers, called the salmon in from great hemispheric journeys, and so testified to the magnetic power of earth on sea. It would be clogged with salmon who sought its narrow, dangerous rivers when they might have stayed in safe salt seas, and the puzzle of their fresh-water expedition grew with the appearance of shad and alewife and ocean-going sturgeon and trout and bass who joined the salmon in their struggle to reach the shore's seductive hills. The western shore drew its fish as though connective tissue pulled them and sought to take them so far inland that they might never return to the sea.

It was also a shore of lobsters and great clam nations, of scattered dominions of oysters and sheltered bays where sardines clustered in fearful anticipation of their enemies. It was a shore of prowling seals and charging swordfish, of basking sharks and tuna hastening by its islands, of cormorants weaving downwind in search of migrant smelt, of codfish browsing on pastures set close inshore.

Its rivers sweetened the salty Gulf and pumped out the chemicals of earth to help sustain the life of the sea. The rivers' influence joined with the turning of the earth, and the Gulf revolved slowly in response to their attentions.

The southern shore of the Gulf was separately distinct. A robin standing in its tallest pine could see a laughing coastline stretching east and west out of sight.

26

Now its bright russet soil was concealed under snow, but the snow could not hide the shore's detachment from the plight of its sister shores. Here, in a trice, the snow could be replaced by gleaming strawberries in parklike fields, by forests lined with flowers, by groves of peas and raspberries spattered throughout its fecund body. Here a robin's song drifted upward to smiling clouds and was caught, transfixed, by the fragile, living tension this shoreline held between the warring north and south.

The Gulf had no soul, but it had a heart, a central core. From this core radiated lines of control which reached into every part of the Gulf. This core was a sunken plateau, a wholly separate place, invisible and submarine, where the cod and haddock teemed, herring and mackerel warred, crab and lobster struggled for their prey, and where the shellfish met the whale. This sunken field, this submerged forest, this rich plateau was formed from the Gulf itself. It was a thief of the island's soil, a borrower of northern fertility, rich in its heartless foreclosure on continental sediment. Surrounded by land, strategically equidistant from every shore, it was the richest place on earth.

IV

The Gulf was a series of invisible highways—submarine, surface, and aerial—along which the Gulf creatures had traveled for thousands of years. Arctic foxes stood on rocking ice pans and came south with the drift. The sea froze and packs of wolves ran out to offshore islands and padded through empty seabird cities. Polar bears, white as winter clouds, came south with the seals and eased voluptuously from pan to pan. They landed on islands, explored the mainland, and returned north, disgusted by the growth of heat.

All the creatures of the Gulf were colonists who had come into it after a final retreat of ice twenty thousand years before, while the destruction of the ice was being repaired. Every speck of dust and vein of leaf, every dragonfly and spring flower, every bird and beast and fish and flagellate had found a place there after the ice had gone. The success or failure of these colonists, old and new, had set the tone for all life in the Gulf.

The lynx reached the big island, and why not? His kind walked free on sea ice. The wolf reached the island too, as well he might, because he found the northern shore hospitable. The caribou made the island journey also, but the raccoon, who seemed so bold, never did. Neither did the skunk. The cougar stopped at the southern strait and looked across that stretch of water to the granite shores. The lynx looked back at him, and both recognized the limits of the other's range. The arctic hare loped across the island easily, commanded it, reached the southern strait, saw the cougar, and stopped. But the straits did not inhibit the varying hares. They crossed them and drove the arctic hare into the mountains before they, in turn, fell under the dominion of the lynx.

All the shores of the Gulf were lined with failures, with creatures who had looked at the water barriers and at the many small islands dotting the Gulf's surface and had stayed where they were, unwilling to make this last colonists' journey. The cowardly woodchucks went nowhere; they dug funkholes and went to sleep in any crisis. The porcupines, who were not cowardly, thrived all along the northern shore but reached none of the islands. They flicked their spines and watched for wolverines. Just as conservative were the red squirrels and the chipmunks and the many shrews and mice and lemmings who clung to mainland security.

But other colonists moved. Muskrats paused for a moment on a beach in the southern Gulf, then plunged into the water and swam offshore, not in response to any special destination but guided by inexplicable sense. They swam hard and some drowned, but others reached islands where they landed and became colonizers. In one ingenious act, it seemed, they had freed themselves from many of their natural enemies. But some of their enemies could

29

swim just as well.

The colonists moved in many ways, leaving footprints when they failed, creating nations when they succeeded. They traveled by air on parachutes or were driven by their propellers. A spider hung on the end of his silken rope could cross the Gulf in a day, and a maple seed might stay an hour in the air as it twirled away in the grip of the wind. The colonists moved in self-contained capsules that held complete life systems, and some could settle down and wait for ten years before resuming the journey. The seeds of trees were able to skip for miles across the winter ice to find new homes. In fact, the trees were as much part of the Gulf as any other life in it, and all were colonists. The personality of each tree determined its placement and its success. The balsam fir, the Gulf's dominant, was aggressive in nature, energetic in habit, yet patient in its capacity to await the right opportunity to spread and survive. When the ice left, the balsam fir pushed north and took over rock-studded mountains with the same ease that it had smothered fertile river valleys. It crossed the southern strait to the big island and pushed north and east, climbing into the mountains, ignoring the resistant soil, less than ten inches deep, clambering up steep mountain sides that drew little sun. The balsam fir made its advance. As a young tree it waited in the shade of others, waited for a break in the canopy, the destruction of its rivals. When that moment came, it leaped to life. Its dense, triangular form shoved its competitors into oblivion and it stood straight in silent triumph for a hundred and fifty years at a time, before senescence and death. This most prolific tree threw out seeds so thickly that any perturbation of the forest saw its progeny rise like manic miniature gladiators, millions of them to every acre. All competition suffocated. Then fir killed fir until only the toughest and strongest survived to make the forest.

All the life forms of the Gulf conformed to the strictures of tradition, but that did not ease their constant pressure to upset the conventional, to replace the old with the new. The balsam fir was never uncontested. Its place on the northern shore, on the highest ground in the west, and on the big island itself was always subject to the hostility of the red spruce. It, too, was a tree that thrived under catastrophe. After hurricanes it sprouted fast and led the race for height. If the land were dry and rocky, it beat everything. It was also patient, and could wait out the fire calamity—wait as the tiny seeds of poplar and birch, light as kisses, blew in from other forests to make their nursery forests; wait while these trees thrived for half a century. Then, at last, the red spruce would expand its columns up through the nursery, past the presuming youth that had seemed so fast, so sure, and its older branches spread and choked.

In the river valleys of the big island, never rich or fertile, the balsam fir spread thickly, but there it was in bitter competition with the black and white spruce and the white birch. In those valleys the red spruce, with its large seeds and its partiality for lowland loam, conceded the territory. There was constant war among the others who did not so concede. Balsam fir fought white spruce, a battle conducted in six inches of sandy soil over pure bedrock. But fir upthrust fifty feet in one hundred years, the birch only thirty.

The silent push and shove of trees on the island was futile counterpoint to the musical wind which got them all in the end anyway. The white birch blew down in the middle of its second hundred years, and balsam fir succumbed to the wind early in its third century.

The island was witness that nothing stopped life from spreading and flowing into every crack and crevice of the body of the Gulf. Every peak and valley, every barren and bog had been invaded. Plants reached and secured places for themselves in parts so inhospitable that the lynx had never seen them. In the high barrens, where a plover's cry died of loneliness and the soil was barely an inch over bedrock, the black spruce triumphed. Its cunning measure of roots spread wide as a mother's arms as it crouched down, prostrate but powerful, insignificant but long-enduring.

The western shore of the Gulf, by contrast, was lush and decadent. It cried out for catastrophe. At all levels of mountain and river valley, its forests had endured too long without change. The gigantic red spruces were like falling generals in the rabble army around them. Forest floors were littered with the debris of centuries of growth, a

32

growth carried on so long that all the trees were tired, intolerant of the security of no change. The western shore needed hurricanes, fires, diseases, anything to end an intolerable old age and bring the fresh new growth of youth.

V

The Gulf, ruler of drift and tide, sent its currents to pump life into every part of its body. The great northern drift, majestically grave and slow, brought a constant arctic transfusion which kept the Gulf vigorously young. It came steadily down the island's shores, brushing aside the feeble outflow of rivers, bending them all south with it. Nothing seemed capable of stopping the drift, which as it entered the northern strait was thirteen hundred feet deep and twenty miles wide, moving irresistibly at one mile an hour. It poured into the Gulf and retained its identity down the western shore of the big island, its speed and power undiminished.

Near the southern strait it began to feel an arm of an oceanic current, born near the equator, which entered the Gulf through the southern strait. The two bodies of water gripped each other angrily. The drift was big enough, powerful enough, surely, to challenge this interloper. The two forces folded into each other and the drift turned left and right as if trying to avoid the challenge. But it was no use. The drift was forced to dive deeply, crushed under the superior strength of the oceanic current, and left behind a surface raging and roaring with the impact of the collision. In the uproar a proliferation of plankton spun and cod leaped and mist boiled constantly from the rupture and defeat of the arctic drift.

The currents were the circulation of the Gulf, its diastole and systole pulsing power through its system. A submarine current, untouched by arctic messages or equatorial interlopers, poured along the bottom of the Gulf, retained in a submarine trench constructed a million years before. It drove against the western shore and raised up strange creatures and odd shades of water before it diffused across the Gulf surface.

The currents collided, and carried life. They seemed so physical, laden with drifting tree seeds and codfish eggs, and juvenile shrimp, and seal armies, and apprehensive foxes. But to the Gulf, in this season, they were unrealized and unheard notes in the spring song to come. The Gulf slept fitfully, slept in memory of that horrific death time of glacial ice. The soil of its shore clanged to the fall of rock and its rivers slept, locked into their landscapes. Among the shore pines of islands the wind tossed white chunks of the Gulf at the comatose earth, and the sea went to sleep when it failed to rouse the shore.

Sleep, passionate sleep, in which the sorrows of time were healed, in which mountains eroded away the glories of old altitudes and the island sent the silts of its youth

34

into the surrounding sea. The Gulf slept, and clung to each grain of soil, held on to its gravels and shales, and dreamed of the time to come. It would be a good time— a caress of herring in calm waters, a cry of gulls, a patience of caribou, a fury of fires, a hornpipe of migration, a carelessness of quick and killing winds, a stillness of spring nights when stars shone on the sleeping eagle. The dream was the soul of the sea and the sound of it striking the shore; it was the music of the Gulf.

Chapter TWO

I

The harp seals opened the spring of the Gulf. They poured into its territory in a great movement that christened the new season with an icy flourish. The Gulf threw out cutting winds and smothering blizzards to ward them off, but the seals were too numerous to be fended away; they were strung out in a careless specking of the sea ice for hundreds of miles.

All winter the seals had moved south on slow-drifting ice, direct messengers from the northern autumn of the previous year when they had begun the journey. Their descent cleared the subarctic of harp seals; it pulled them off the coasts of islands and out of fiords and glacier bays; it took them from ice packs and icebergs and brought them down into the Gulf in one great migration, millions strong.

The Gulf tried to remain aloof to their entry, but the ice could not ignore them. Its grip on the northern Gulf, once paralyzing, was weakened with the arrival of the seals. It could not maintain its cohesion against such an invasion. Sharp rifts and breaks flashed through its corporation. Simultaneously, winter-weary sea dwellers saw the seals darting through the black water, or sensed them nearby, and surrendered. The seals must clean up those who had survived the winter only through luck. Each day of the seals' advance these victims were sacrificed to the migration.

The entrance of the seals shocked the Gulf, and it stirred. Teeth rent flesh; a long stain of blood spread outward from the seal army. The movement of the harps was fluid and unpredictable. One morning they were gone completely from the ice; they were at sea, hunting. The next day they appeared in a score of big divisions to doze on the ice. The females, now ten months pregnant, were hungry and anxious not to be diverted from their assignment in the Gulf. They stood on the edge of the ice, muzzles lifted and whiskers drooping, and looked south as the ice clanged and ground around them. The older ones remembered that this could be a time of disaster, not merely for a few thousand creatures caught in the ice and crushed, but for whole nations wrecked at the point of fruition, with the dead and dying strewn around so ruthlessly it was as though the Gulf had declared that it, too, could be as rigorous as the arctic.

The seals came down into the Gulf during days flushed bright with a white hard sun shining on peaks of ice. Ivory gulls, following the seals south, whispered to each other. The white eagle hung at an immense height over the strait and saw ice jamming together, heard its groaning and wheezing as its body was broken up inside. He remembered that this often meant red meat laid out on the ice for him, but as he watched, a long black scar ran across the ice and thousands of seals moved toward it. While he circled, they disappeared into the water.

II

Before the seal nation could escape from the northern strait, the Gulf attacked a final time. A storm struck as the seals' rear guard, some three million creatures compressed into a hundred-mile-long train, was being expelled by the strait. The storm swung in from the eye of the morning sun, a perfect whiteout of brilliant light amid the fleeing ice crystals. The seals huddled down, becoming invisible as the white mass clung to their coats. Vision was distorted, twisted, tantalized. In a rift in the whiteout, the unmoving ice seemed to billow like waves and the supine seals to dance.

The wind increased, brittle as fallen ice. The snow touched the edge of the ice pack and fled in frozen fragments. A group of small seabirds, dovekies driven two days in the wind, lost all resistance and surrendered to its force. Wing bones snapped as they were carried over the ice pack; limp bodies quickly froze to contorted corpses. The sky, dark as ruffled velvet, enclosed the ice which reared, grinding and telescoping, in response to the breathless haste of the wind.

Dark, hesitant shapes lay on the ice pack in the murk of the driven snow. The seals were made uncertain by the movement of the ice; they knew the menace of moving pans and the danger of the dark water. Suddenly resolute, some dived and ice pans crunched together above them. They were safe, but the closure of the ice was becoming general, and later the seals' eyes appeared at odd transparent ice-patch windows in their submarine prison. Suffocating, they longed now for the uncertainty of the ice surface.

The wind built cumulative power and crunched the ice tighter, wrenching from it a mortal groan. Abruptly the ice broke in a series of long pleats; massive folds jumped skittishly to the top of the pack. Some slid, and the tons flattened the pack surface smooth as obsidian. The wind screamed and more piles of ice rose to conquer the resistance of the pack. Majestic in their rise, they teetered at the elbow of a group of seals. The seals looked in oblique surprise for frozen moments, then the ice fell, drawing from their white tombs long streams of blood which froze immediately in question marks.

The wind was not without humor; it proffered death here, salvation there. It drove seabirds mercilessly, pushed them as far as they would go, then wrecked them. A flock of murres, immaculate and tight-coated, appeared suddenly and fell into the lea of a minor mountain of upthrust ice. The wind lost its grip on their wings and dropped to a murmur. The birds keened like dogs in the black air. Panic-stricken, they knew one thing well: they must reach open sea to ride out the winter. They rose together, saved, but the wind's humor changed, and a blast laughed them across the ice, away from the sea. The way west, in the storms of this season, was choked with ice; there was no water open anywhere in strait, or bay, or inlet. The murres, desperate, forgot the necessity of open water and skeltered west. Dropouts crashed on the ice and heard the ripping sounds of gyrfalcons' wings overhead. Snowy owls stood on ice hills, impassive observers. Later, when the storm was over, the murres looked up and saw a white eagle descending in leisurely, confident circles.

III

The shore appeared at this dawn grim and inhospitable, a place of alarm and disaster, the division point between the frozen earth of the north and the captive waters of the south.

40

Willow ptarmigans came out of a pallid overcast, their plumage winter-white. They were heading south and would have outrun the gradual failure of northern food if the Gulf shore had not revealed itself and become a deflection point. The ptarmigans' flight was bent and turned west in the wake of the murres. Scattered birds appeared at first, then a flock weaving shades of gray and white above the ice and black rock spires of the shore, and were gone in minutes. Flight after flight appeared and amalgamated to fight the driving blusters. For half a day the sky was filled with these northerners searching for survival at the Gulf.

The ptarmigan flights drowned out the sounds of other travelers. These others, tiny maroon-crowned redpolls, moved quiet as kindness through the birches and poplars and cedars and tamaracks and pines. They were heading west, but the redpolls were not panicky refugees; they were circumpolar wanderers who moved free in space and time with no permanent address. They knew the Gulf and made no move to cross it. This winter they had already passed an arctic sea and hunted the edge of the tundra and the scree-slashed slopes above old glaciers. Their twittering cries, thin and ethereal as reeds, piped in the wind of the subarctic deserts. They undulated and dropped into clearings in search of seeds. Now they were moving west before they went north again, up toward the roof of the world, and then on to another continent.

The ptarmigans and redpolls passed on, swallowed in cold air, and the Gulf ignored their departure. The shore was swept clear of fliers as if in readiness for the next flight, and it came almost immediately. The dovekies invited retaliation from the winter because of their extraordinary abundance. They strengthened the invitation by their reaction to the worst of the wind and ice. Caught by a gale in a sheltered leashore position near the northern strait, they rushed west and hit the northern Gulf shore in a straggling, disorderly rabble. The few remaining ptarmigans unobtrusively filtered into the hinterlands, skulking in clearings along river valleys.

For sixteen days dovekies roared along the Gulf shore, a seemingly endless passage of birds—millions upon millions, in rustling preoccupied flights. Possessed by demons, they were driven on the wings of a panic that would last for days, until sanity returned and they would begin filtering east again, back through the strait, back to an island of snow, of great cliffs and glistening glaciers—their summer breeding home.

IV

The lynx watched the shore, wise from other years. The point of tension between land and sea was where the resolution of sea creatures collapsed and they dropped, sought mercy from the land. The lynx was there to see they did not get it.

A group of murres landed, confused, and ran back

42

and forth. Some of them jumped aloft and headed west, always west, although the wind was down. Easy for them to have returned east, to the safety of the arctic water, but instead they played out their tiny, tragic, western drama.

The lynx's eyes glowed. He mistrusted all open territory, but he came out of the trees and crossed the beach. The saturnine birds, feeding their panic, stumbled and jostled one another. At the approach of the lynx a few of them took off. Some would end up in the continental basin and be among the cheerful redpolls, and there, baffled by a place they did not know, would die as the redpolls danced away free.

The lynx jumped.

Longspurs, wanderers like the redpolls, loved the tundra and bare glacial hills but they were dubious about this Gulf land. Their arrival rippled the air with whistling cries, and their light bodies danced in a pale white sky, circling a northern shore island for an hour and thickening at midday until the sky seemed an inverted bowl to hold their music. Their grace and the light movement of their wings suggested harmony and an ecstacy at variance with the grim urgency of the previous travelers. The long shore seemed lighter and gayer in their presence.

But their appearance indicated failure elsewhere. They were not meant to be concentrated like this. They were creatures of the open spaces with their flocks well dispersed. Many of them hastened across the strait and supplicated the big island.

The lynx understood their plight and waited as they

settled the shore. He could smell a change in the air. The gale that struck the shore that night might have been at his invitation. The rain came down first and the temperature jumped back and forth between freezing and thawing so that the rain hit the trees, congealed, unable to act either as water or as ice. The wind fingered deeply into the lynx's fir forest and he padded under the longspur's dormitory. In the early morning a few thousand longspurs shook ice off their wings and blundered away through the trees. None could fly well in the wind. Their awkward flight and piping cries sent the lynx running, and the rest of the birds roused from frozen apathy to a general panic. The lynx jumped and fell, empty-pawed. The trees chattered with falling ice. Wings flickered to the sound of bird cries and failed flight. The lynx crouched, elbows upthrust, and ate.

At dawn, the freeze ascendant, a great longspur mortality lingered in the forest. Victims lay with their wings akimbo, patching snow white and brown, and the bloated lynx ate on.

He ate, and was oblivious to the departure of the survivors who rose in the dawn light, not crying, and were gone into the west. He ate, and ravens came down through the trees and joined in the feast. He ate, and snowy owls drifted overhead and the white eagle appeared. As the feast continued, thin flocks of snow buntings fled against the distant scrub pine, inheritors of some tiny sense that made them immune to such an accident in the Gulf.

V

The humor of the wind was black and its roars and moans were bombast in the night. Then it fell to a gray whisper and the ice sighed, releasing its tense corporation so that in places black water-rifts showed, from which, lungs bursting, seals appeared.

But behind them, the wind was laughing; it was as strong as ever. Some seals died slowly, jammed in a closing rift that took its time. The seals added their voices to the wind and their cries united with the memories of stricken dovekies, the wingbeats of extinct murres, and the panic of a million dead longspurs.

The desolation of the dawn held piercing beauty. The design traced by the night wind was exquisite and complex on the face of the ice. The new world was utterly arctic and blindingly white. It swept into myriad sharp peaks of snow which smoked at their crests and caught the glow of a pink sun which intruded hesitantly, was blown out, intruded again, and shook at the vast view of ice.

The ice pack opened up, and the seals, having eaten out the northeastern corner of the Gulf, leaped off the ice and disappeared into the water. The ice ride was over. Some of them headed due south, at high speed, and reached the southern Gulf, hundreds of miles away, in two

45

days. There they lolled in coastal water and ate shellfish and scooped up sleepy herring. Other seals appeared in the estuaries of western shore rivers and tested continental waters, leaving them in disgust to foray up and down the shore. An army of them came out of the sea suddenly off the southern shores of the big island and decimated a population of unwary codfish.

In the shallows everywhere, the seals found flounder, easy to catch in this season. The year before, the giant cod had been in the southern Gulf shallows when the seals arrived. He found the sea uncomfortable with their snaking bodies and snapping jaws, and had fled into deeper water.

But deep water was no refuge from these hungry creatures. They came among great winter gatherings of capelin and struck among them, smashing their tight cohesion. They drove some schools into very deep water or split them into a dozen smaller schools and then destroyed them.

The seals turned south and west and fell among winter haddock in the middle deeps, and harried them. They found sculpins along the southeastern shore of the mainland and shrimp in very deep water; in places they dived five hundred feet to reach their food. They fished for haddock on the edge of the sunken central plateau and harassed salmon loitering close inshore along the island.

The lobster, eye stalks rigid and tail sucked under his belly in sudden apprehension, watched the panoply of passing seals and heard fortress walls being smashed around him. His torpid fear quickened his blue blood and his own walls quaked, shook, shivered.

The hunting seals feasted and grew fat, and the end of their southern trip was near. In some mysterious way the waters of the Gulf carried a message that was communicated to every seal. It flashed the full length of the western shore, all around the Gulf, and the seals moved commonly, so intent on their single purpose that no creature was left behind or remained uninformed of the mission. Back to the ice, back to the sketchy mid-Gulf hunting, all the creatures up onto the ice, cool and clear, all up now, bellyflopped, heads up, questioning, belly-bulging, up out of the dripping dark water, up out of the Gulf.

Now it was spring, though the Gulf still denied it; spring, though snow pelted the seals; spring, though the southern shallows were freezing again. No matter, the seals whelped.

Millions of pups, white-haired, with large and mournful eyes, looked up. Whiskers drooped as they suckled the richest milk on earth. Each pup's weight grew five times in fourteen days. At ninety pounds the pups looked around them, but they were alone. Mothers slipped away forever into the Gulf; they were gone, and the pups' dark eyes looked out and the whiskers drooped, but their questions lay stillborn on ice pans. Half the weight given them by that incredible mother's milk was fat, and this they consumed. Their white coats shed quickly on the ice, and a new gray-black blotched coat appeared. With equal speed, their permanent teeth pushed through their gums, and now, armed and heavily coated, they were ready to leave

47

the ice, enter the Gulf, and begin independent lives. The Gulf, defeated by this success, could only feign its sleep.

VI

The ice might bear down, it might crush bodies and wills, but it reached only a few of the creatures of the winter Gulf. It was a gift to the Gulf, not a shroud, and under it creatures slept off its presence, oblivious to the passage of ice, the arrival of seals, the hints of a changing season. Blue-eyed scallops littered the shallow bottom here, unmoving in the gloom, eyes tight shut behind armored walls, insensitive to passing fish, to the crunch of shells broken in seal jaws, to the tint of blood in dusky water.

Packed under rocks, in meandering reefs of stone, wedged between boulders buried in limp dead weeds, lobsters waited out the ice torment, eye stalks vigilant but antennae still. Crabs pulled feet tight against their shells and waited, and oysters slept securely, feeding on starch stored the previous year, their heartbeats slowed, all growth stopped, the whole winter passing without loss of weight.

Ice commanded the Gulf, but did not rule it. Ice claimed dominion, but possessed no territory. The hollow cries of evening grosbeaks and wandering crossbills, the chattering of nuthatches and chickadees proclaimed the

48

forest's unconcerned acceptance of the ice. Juncoes drifted among tall white pine and left forked white bars behind them, and a storm of snow buntings hurtled along the southern shore in search of a fire-wrought clearing, a mountain slope sprouting dry seed heads from the snow.

Trees were as unconcerned by the seal drama as the Gulf itself. Branches groaned under the weight of snow, but the trees were not diminished by the snap and crackle of breaking limbs, the quick rushes of falling snow among their branches. Poplars and birches, maples and iron-woods, alders and beeches, oaks and elms, witch hazels and mountain ashes, cherries and sumacs, all asleep and facing the ice naked. Snow fell among their empty limbs and plastered their trunks. The echo of the robin's trou-badour song clung so faintly in their congregations that it was scarcely even a memory.

The forests swept down into the valleys, into mean-dering rivers, into streams and ponds, into landbound arteries in the meeting halls of the Gulf. Dark shadows fell across the arctic char waiting under ice, and touched keen brook trout facing downrushing black water. On the mud lay the ounaniche, landlocked salmon, slow-growing lake dwellers well adjusted now to being forever prisoners of the land. The shadows came down through dark water and fell among eels buried in mud and awaiting a separate assignment in the sea. They touched the smelt waiting un-der estuary ice, while, nearby, young expectant winter flounder felt the excitement of the seals and made one hesitant movement toward the shore.

49

The creatures of the Gulf outwaited the ice, and outlived it, and looked through this blizzard at the lynx, whose eyes were caked with snow as he peered uselessly for a glimpse of the fleet hare. The white-tailed deer gathered in the driven snow, and in sheltered places bear breath columned out of snow holes among the trees, and the tracks of careful cougars wound from dusk till dawn. The caribou chewed a hopeful forest to death.

Chapter THREE

I

Seals heralded the spring and the giant cod responded to their dwindling barks. He left the bottom, knowing he belonged at the surface although no warming current or brightening light had reached him. He moved up through the monotone of the middle depths, a spaceship poised between two worlds. He knew the spring; he knew about the retreating seals, and his knowledge was shared by others around him. All moved toward the surface of the Gulf.

Yet the Gulf, stubborn now, held back. The ice pans had gone and so had the seals, but the winds were cold as truth. The cod grew hungry as he swam inside waves which glittered with yellow foam and were as empty as his own belly. But the codfish knew this sea, and he felt the spring, though the water around him appeared empty.

And the codfish was right. The visible spring had begun five hundred miles away in a sheltered bay midway up the western shore, a visible spring born of the gales which had pushed all of the Gulf against that shore. The waves in which the codfish swam creamed on west and leaned hard against the western shore, trapped thousands of waves inside that bay, broke up the smug temperature layers constructed so carefully during the winter, and created a common consistency and temperature from the bottom to the top of the coastal waters.

The waves crashed on the western shore, and their determination brought an elixir of spring up from the bottom, a chemical mix dumped there by coastal rivers, formed there by the dissolution of the dead during the long cold season. This life-giving brew was swirled in every wave. It spread across the surface of the Gulf. The sea began to grow.

The cod swam in the foaming surface. The pulse of the sea pulled and pushed at him. It told him of the transformation now close, told him that the season was for him. He let himself swing away west in a breaking wave. The Gulf was ready for the march of the plankton.

No other army ever mustered such dashing, peculiar soldiers, or such numbers of them—enough, untrammeled, to cover the earth in a few days; a swelling of creatures and plants together, unified into dominions, commonwealths, nations, empires all interconnected and interdependent. Some groups were passive plebeians accepting of fate; others, barbarian hordes raging to be off and pillaging. Behind them came further rushes of populations, each following the other in predictable order.

The giant cod waited. He knew about this growth of the plankton empire and was to join in its many days of expansive activity. Dark shapes rose around him, flicked tails, and waited with him. The waves hissed impatiently, and from out of nowhere the first diatom, a microscopic plant, appeared.

The cod might face a thousand diatoms and see nothing. He was linked to them, but the chain was too long for his perception. The diatom, too early for this place, died, and the cod waited on. A second diatom materialized, then a million of them, and dematerialized just as quickly as they consumed and exhausted the small traces of phosphates and nitrates in the water. Their eagerness had tested the central Gulf and found it deficient. But the diatoms of the western shore found what they needed, and the revolution began.

They had endured the winter dormant, near to death, like seeds awaiting the sprout of spring as they drifted back and forth or rolled in sand and mud and gravel. Each diatom was a chloroplast imprisoned in a silica house, the shell for protection, the chloroplast an engine to transform the energy of the sunlight into new, life-making substances. Up they came, out they went, brown protoplasmic bodies tinting the water. In the mass they were brown, but in detail they were a sparkle of colors, like gems cast carelessly through the water. Crystal spots gleamed in the sun. Amber necklaces drooped languidly. Arrow-shaped diatoms shafted. Scintillant joined emeralds floated in tiny seas of their own making. Each diatom worked on some variation of a common theme: the division of a single cell again and again for as long as the Gulf provided the food and the light. Sheets of golden creatures waved a greeting to the tumult of the diatom crowd.

The giant cod waited in his still-empty sea.

The silica shells split and diatoms divided a billion times, and walls grew between the shells, and two plants moved off. The phosphates and nitrates, well stirred up now, impregnated the water, and the entire western shore became a bacchanal of dividing cells, and the water was brown and slimy in quiet places.

This was a true, sustaining spring. The seal spring had been exploitive. From the diatoms, the first plankton members, sprang all sea life. The cod could wait confidently now for a series of sympathetic explosions that eventually would bring a flood of life to his nose, and he would feast. The inshore diatoms and other plants expanded; the southern shore took up the task, and thick-shelled bottom-dwelling diatoms awoke and divided, and everywhere the upsurge of life was infectious. Diatoms clashed the phosphates and nitrates together and the great island was surrounded by new diatom nations. Even the bleak northern shore came alive with them, and the life reaction reached into the center of the Gulf.

54

II

The giant cod rolled in a wave, but now it was full. Hungry herring rushed at him, darkened the water, broke the surface, and he went mad. The herring knew about the diatoms precisely, and their appearance presaged an upsurge of the rest of the plankton, that incredible conglomeration of tiny plants and animals, eggs, and larvae, enough to feed the enormous corporate appetite of the herring. Their knowledge of this time and place made them oblivious, and the cod, transformed into a dancing fool of a fish, slashed and chopped and gobbled at their unresponsive mass. The diatoms grew under dim skies, clouds ran west, chill winds took wave tops aloft, and more cod poured up from the bottom. The chain reaction—from the wind to the bottom of the sea, from the sun to the dividing cell, from the herring to the cod's belly—was for the moment complete. The cod drifted, his belly distended.

The cod could now be sure of continuous surface hunting until the fall of the diatoms. A quarter of a century of experience told him that the diatoms had their specific cycle. They would eat out some regions of the Gulf surface, make them almost sterile, and, with the elixir gone, would become insensible or dead from lack of it. The sun would shine with growing cheer, but with the salts gone and the herring spread out more thinly at the surface in search of new hunting, too fast, too diffuse for the cod to follow, he would sink again to the bottom. In some years, caught in such regions, he accompanied the rain of dying diatoms falling to the bottom through layers of temperature to lay down carpets of invisible corruption that would be transformed by bacteria. The sterile water would await the next overturn of the sea, the gales of fall, and the sun of the following spring which would create another feast at the surface—and presage the next famine.

The diatoms led the way. Behind them came another wave of plants, the flagellates, also close to the start of life; in them were contained hints of higher life. Their forms were no more diverse than the diatoms, but they were more ingenious, less geometric. Expressed in a profusion of circular shapes, some were spined in star form, others molded like hearts. All were equipped with an extraordinary contribution to the evolution of life. The flagella was a long whip which lashed them into action, drove them up into the now-warming surface waters, and kept them there.

The flagellates thickened around the dancing cod as he ate the herring who were eating the flagellates. Unconcerned, the flagellates divided. They had solved one problem that plagued the diatoms. Each diatom division produced one plant smaller than the original until their diminishing size became unbearable and they rejected their silica houses entirely. They formed burgeoning chunks of protoplasm, fashioned new and larger shells around the protoplasm, and started the divisive process once more. But as the flagellates divided they kept their sizes equal. Some of them could shuck their shells and grow new ones; others had light-sensitive organs—perhaps the first eyes on earth—with tiny lenses and pigment cups. Some had within their still-invisible bodies the capacity to make light—a mystery, this, for all the sea to watch. Later in the year the giant cod would sail under a sea surface illuminated by millions of pinpricks of light, his passage through the Gulf accompanied by great corporate flashings and glowings.

III

The plants staked out new fields and looked invulnerable, so vast were their numbers, until the copepods appeared in every part of the Gulf at once, an indication of a fast-maturing spring. This was the beginning of the crustacean rush into the Gulf, and the copepods were followed by commonwealths of ostracods and decapods, by mysids and amphipods, by quadrillions of crablike, shrimplike, crawfishlike creatures whose numbers diminished the records set by the diatoms. Ultimately they became the most numerous creatures in the Gulf, and in the world.

The copepods came out of deep water. They had been

drifting everywhere in the Gulf, fat from the previous year and feeding throughout the winter on this fat. Now they rose to the blooming surface and rushed ahead. The giant cod, still hunting, saw them coming, each one pinhead-sized, with body and head in one piece, decorated with long trailing antennae and terminated by a long, forked, waving tail. Up they came, warlike limbs thrusting them past the silent cod's nose. They possessed what the flagellates had only suggested; they each had one eye, a single orb placed in the middle of the head, three lenses in each eye, a cup of dark pigment behind, each eye powered by a separate nerve to the brain. Two of the three lenses looked forward and upward; the third looked downward. They waved their antennae and drove currents toward their mouths, filtering a continuous vegetable meal.

This copepod success was as suspect as that of the diatoms. They invited the anti-host, and got it. The Gulf allowed no sudden, unrestricted abundance. The cod was enveloped by transparent, practically invisible arrow-worms. They teemed in the southern strait, poured into the Gulf toward the copepod complex. Tails lashing, they advanced up the western shore. They fired themselves through the northern Gulf and clusters of bristles in their heads gaped wide and clamped down on copepod bodies. Their tiny black eyes glistened, and these eyes were the only ones on earth which saw in every direction at once. Three segmented divisions in each orb faced forward, backward, upward, and downward. These eyes peered back and down through the worms' own transparent bodies to

58

consider which copepod to annihilate next. The arrow-worms spread, rampaged, and slaughtered, and the giant cod cruised a misty shore.

He passed through miles of arrow-worms, now visible with the copepods stuffed inside them; now they were hunted and snapped up singly by herring as the stately cod moved on, belly bulging. A swallowed copepod looked with a single eye through the wall of his worm-captor's stomach and saw the next victim loom up as the worm fired himself six times the length of his body in attack, and then felt the new victim nestling against his own body, awaiting digestion.

In the southern Gulf a small creature of the plankton hordes appeared, an oikopleura, just visible with a tadpole tail waving and possessed of its own notion of survival. The giant cod sank into a greening canyon which danced with broken shafts of light as the oikopleuras built houses with secretions of thin, gelatinous materials. Each house was fitted with two hatches that were covered by a fine, netlike mesh. Inside were even finer sets of nets. The oikopleuras positioned themselves under the hatch holes and wriggled their tails vigorously among the flagellates and copepods and arrow-worms. The currents of water drawn through the hatch holes brought food with them, food that was caught in the nets and then passed to the mouths of the oikopleuras. If danger threatened, the oikopleuras fled. They slipped through escape hatches at the backs of their houses and became invisible at once in the green water. Later, the danger gone, the gelatin flowed again and set, and new houses were built, and the oikopleuras resumed hunting.

IV

A Gulf consisting of endless plankton fields suggested many other levels of life, and they were there. Hollow-gutted coelenterates, circled by tentacles, appeared in billions, the only creatures in the Gulf to use poison darts to bring down their prey. Stinging cells, flipped inside out when they were grazed or jolted, presented spines which cut into the bodies of victims. Hollow needles were fired into the wounds, a paralyzing drug injected. The giant codfish drifted, a majestic dirigible among these subtle miniatures, and remained forever a stranger to their ingenuity. Often they mounted their artillery in batteries and fired their needles in unison. Some, perhaps refined by experience, did not bother to sting their prey. Instead, the victim was entangled in tentacles and stuck to adhesive pads.

The Gulf was in a flux of new life, but the submarine fields were bloody rather than verdant. The ctenophores appeared, fragile and beautiful. The giant cod saw them clearly when the sun caught and refracted in prismatic waves through their globe bodies. They were comb jellies, transparent spheres riddled with a system of canals and trailing long, diaphanous tentacles. They looked innocent until the mouth at the bottom of each ctenophore sphere opened; they looked insensate until the fringes of cilia which propelled them rippled down the hemispheres and sent them moving off.

The ctenophores massed over the plateau in the central Gulf, in the southern strait, and in the southern Gulf shallows. Like fishermen they flung out long lines that twisted and turned in the water and were adhesive to the touch and instantly lethal to any member of the plankton empire. The diatoms fell to the ctenophores' attack in countless numbers. When the knobs on the tentacles were nicely loaded with them, the ctenophores twirled their bodies, winding in the tentacles until their mouths could reach and eat the harvest.

The ctenophores moved among larval herring who were eating diatoms, and the hunting became a confrontation between creatures of nearly equal size. The ctenophores needed guile to subdue the small herring. The herring, caught and held, pulled the ctenophores back and forth as the lasso-like cells entangled them more closely. The ctenophores fought back. Each one extended and contracted the length of his tentacle, playing with the fish until it tired, then rolled his body until the fish was at the mouth, and eaten.

The giant cod floated and the warriors of the plankton swarmed at his flanks. He was unaware that the herring being eaten now were meals deprived to him later. Some herring, fighting hard, would not submit to the approaching mouth of the ctenophore. They wrenched the tentacle free and swam off with it. But most were eaten. The luckiest ctenophores bulged with the herring packed like cordwood inside their globular bodies. They were fully visible now, and the giant cod snapped up a few of them.

In the shank of one afternoon, sky bright and blue, clouds racing, the ctenophores of the plateau finished eating a herring nation and decimated other plankton there. When night came they celebrated. The sea became a light show, and the giant cod watched, but without sensitivity to the puzzle. A swarm of flashing lights dotted the sea, illuminating it with a steady glow, and the giant cod's gleaming sides gave off burnished reflections of the ctenophores' show and his eyes glowed with their light, and then the ctenophores moved off toward the southern moon.

V

The plankton world warred on, an attrition of populations at every level of the Gulf sea. The plants pirouetted toward the sun and the animals came hastening after them, slaughtering them, and the plants fell from grace and the animals were masters, but their fall came, too, in starvation or in the mouths of bigger hunters. Medusae, apparently blind and helpless, collided with larval barnacles and deftly twisted themselves so that their mouths could engulf the barnacles. The medusae floated on, hollow-bodied, one end splayed like an open umbrella. Some trailed wavering lines, some had decorated, baroque fili-grees, some wore geometric collars. Others, lethal-looking, had spherical bodies containing grim orange machines whose struts and bars held up crafty central engines. They were shaped like great wheels, like the undersides of mushrooms, like hollow bullets.

The spring of the sea ended abruptly. The last of the diatoms, late-thriving in the northern strait, came to an end, and a sigh of regret passed through the Gulf. The giant cod sank, disappeared into purple water. The elixir was exhausted everywhere. The Gulf received the falling victims, disintegrating bodies, tentacles, silica shells drop-ping invisibly to the bottom, some containing the dead, others holding creatures withdrawn into the waiting time when wind or temperature changes would stir up the sea, and they, like the seals, would once again race into view and impregnate the Gulf.

Chapter FOUR

I

While the plankton empire was expanding in the sea, the Gulf came fully awake. To waken from such sound sleep strained every speck of its matter: black rocks, filled with ice, exploded and threw debris down cliff sides; rivers snapped like whips as they cracked the white scab ice and moved miles of it downstream; pus-colored water gushed out of the ice, too impatient to await its thawing, and slithered downhill to the sea. Shorelines howled as ice, freed from its grip on coast rocks, pulled skin and flesh out to sea and dumped it offshore.

The awakening sent pain shooting through all extremities. Bleared eyes focused; reluctant blood pushed to the farthest reaches of the corporation. Numb earth found it was alive and endured the pain to reach the ecstacy of being truly awake. Beyond the awakening was a flushed awareness of rivers rumbling their delight at the sky, of beaches hastily re-forming in familiar symmetries, of trees standing tall and tides rising free and the waters of spring running fast.

The ice broke up. Bears lurched into the open in search of water. The Gulf's great body moved groggily. Deep in the mountains and southern lowlands of the big island the last blizzard of winter had isolated the caribou and starved the lynx, impoverished the wolves and blasted the central lakes with drifts, but this mischief was undone swiftly. The crunch of moving ice and the hiss of melting snow signaled the arctic char, resident over winter in the lakes. They began a rush for the sea as though the island were contaminated. They fled in a great downward movement, a series of free falls, heedless over weirs and waterfalls and rapids, a roar and a hiss between silent spruce, a splash of white-and-yellow water. They would sea hunt into the autumn. Then, tired of the sea, they would return to the river of their birth to spawn.

Fifteen hundred miles away the grilse arrowed forward, due west across the hemisphere.

The rivers of the Gulf were highways traveled in either direction; they lured those who had wintered at sea and now needed a refuge in which to breed. The exuberant smelt had waited under estuarine ice in many parts of the Gulf for this moment, and they smelled the thaw and were transformed. It sent them off, mad for the moment. They threw themselves upriver in solid columns, choked rivulets with their bodies, and were buffeted by downcoming ice, contributing a mass sacrifice to the notion of immortality. As they reached their many destinations in scores of rivers, their hastening hordes thinned; streams branched and rebranched; they swam in fast shallows and under fallen trees and through masses of winter-fallen underbrush to where streams ended in hollows and at crystal bubblings from earth. They stopped and milled in brush-covered pools high in the hills.

The smelts tasted snow shaken from spruce fronds and felt the earth moving beneath them as it thawed. Their anxiety to reach as deep as possible into the substance of the earth breached the arteries of the Gulf and made the rivers ready for the alewives, creatures of more sober mien. The alewives did not intend to take the insane risks of the smelts. Some had already entered the Gulf and mingled with the smelts in estuaries, awaiting the touch of spring, but they could not bring themselves to push upriver so early. Instead they loitered for a while, indecisive, and finally spawned in nearby ponds and lakes and were soon spent.

The grilse, traveling night and day, reached the shores of the big island and he too smelled spring flushed down the rivers. He faced toward the taste of mountains, gills working hard. But these were alien rivers, and he could not enter them.

66

The spent alewives waited. Behind them, but ahead of the grilse, the main body of the alewife armies entered the Gulf. They came en masse through the southern strait and headed immediately for meetings with a score of rivers on the western shore. They were the virgins, four-year-olds who knew nothing except the imperative of passing seconds; all were anxious to find fast-running tributaries tumbling into larger rivers.

The grilse joined a flicker of cod rushing ahead of him, and with them he chased away gloomy night shadows. Ahead lay a river, a torrent, a waterfall, a supreme test. The cod flickered and were gone.

The spawning of the alewives was less the end of a migration than the beginning of a run from which there was no escape. While the grilse was safe in deep rock-punctured coastal waters, the alewives ran like fools. Not cautious now, they showed their backs to the pallid sun and went inland in a flight that would last almost without pause until the fall. Fertility made everything possible, and from it evolved an absurd but true proposition: young lives thrown carelessly against old hills would eventually wear down the hills. The alewives hit every river on the western and southern Gulf shores. Two hundred arteries swelled with their optimistic presence.

Clots of gulls hovered over them when they surfaced in estuaries, but they dived before the gulls could catch them. The gulls waited and they came up again, and went down again until the bite of fresh water caught them and they came up again, and they no longer cared if they were at the surface or not. The gulls knew all about alewives, and waited at every shallow bar and at the mouth of every tributary leading into larger rivers. They hovered over every shallow run of water. They reached down, plucked up thousands of fish, swallowed them, vomited, swallowed again, and were sent into the sky screaming as the press of urgent, foolish fish swept their feet from under them. Fragments from alewife bodies littered river beaches and mudbanks, but no amount of dying slowed the inland march.

The white eagle was there. He knew the alewives as well as the gulls; he had come south to be with them. He landed in the teeming shallows in an angry sprawl of wing and talon, neck feathers hooded, to scatter wading fish crows whose delight in alewives was greater than their fear of eagles. For days the white eagle worked his way up one river and into a stream, and saw the water black with bodies and pools heaving with squirming fish. Later he would see herons spearing the fish and raccoons abroad in daylight scooping up alewives in the shallows. Later still, fat and clumsy after his eating, he would become bored with alewives and return to the earth where the taste of flesh told of richer blood.

Behind him he would leave a spawning that had become monotonous in its repetition though the players changed from time to time. The flood of eggs would draw the perch and pickerel to the spawning grounds. As the alewives reeled back and their eggs hatched, kingfishers would drop down to take their share. Eels would shrug

68

clear of night mud and gather in slimy black ropes to gorge themselves in pools kicking with larval alewives.

II

The grilse reached the southern strait and felt the conflict in the currents, but this was not the time for hesitation. The sea moved with other grilse, and he moved with them.

The spawning fish traveled the river highways in search of a dream. The grilse reached a shore bent with rocks and smothered in clinging weeds. At his shoulder were large shad, two feet long, with twisting, powerful tails which sent them pushing on ahead. The shad moved by the hundreds of thousands rather than by the alewife millions, and their deliberate manners harmonized with the personalities of the rivers they sought: pacific, broad, mature. Before the grilse even reached the western shore of the Gulf, some of the shad were three hundred miles inland and swimming strongly for their places, rashes of tributaries falling into big rivers, sandy, gravelly bottoms where their prolific egg-casting would give their young over to the mercy of the falling water.

In this sequence of spawning fish, punctiliously acted out, the Gulf was ready for the salmon, the royal spawners. The Gulf belonged to them now. Their movement did not resemble the urgent thrust of the alewife masses; it was, rather, an infusion of fish spread across the full width of the Gulf. Salmon drifted into the Gulf through the northern strait. They loitered along the western shore of the big island. They flooded across the southern Gulf shallows.

Halfway across the shallows the grilse paused, his appetite diminished as he felt the call of the river very strong in him. He found himself among others of his kind, but scarcely any of them were from his sea territory. Some had spent all their time at sea in the Gulf itself. Some had grown to maturity in deep waters three hundred miles east of the island near a bleak glacial land never fully recovered from the last ice age. Others came from the edge of the northern ice pack, and they swam with fish who had grown up in another hemisphere. Of all sizes and ages, they agreed on only one fact; they must reach the river where they had been born, perhaps even find the same gravels where, as eggs, they had been hatched.

As the grilse waited in the southern Gulf shallows, now not sure of his direction or purpose, yet another group of salmon passed him. These fish knew what they were doing; they were the mature spawners of previous years, familiar with their rivers, in superb physical condition, fat, blue-black-silver, confident. They disappeared west across the shallows and the grilse drifted hesitantly after them. Elsewhere this nation of early-maturing adults had already encircled the big island and, at a signal, headed inland.

Simultaneously, others of their group struck home

70

all along the northern shore, and the white eagle, reliable watcher, dropped from his sky hook and stood overlooking his favorite salmon river. He knew something about fish exhausted by spawning. The salmon struck in all along the western shore. In ten days about two million of them left the sea for fresh water. They were not heedless, not reckless; they had none of the foolishness of the alewives, little of the push of the smelt and shad, but they were determined, and moved almost cautiously, mostly at night, and sought the sanctuary of one pool after another. They often spent long moments on the bottom, fins barely moving, before another upstream surge.

The grilse left the southern shallows and pushed west as fast as possible, not stopping for food.

III

As the adult pioneers moved inland, the silent, intent lynx watched them in the night shallows of the island. The creaming rivers freshened with the last of the melting snow from the highest ground, and simultaneously a flood of smolts—young salmon—filled the rivers. Born three years previously, they had changed from their freckled, troutlike appearance to lean, silver-scaled, big-eyed explorers at the beginning of journeys that might end in another hemisphere. They moved out of the high streams

71

and rivers everywhere around the Gulf and, for a moment, the land mourned their passing. The Gulf, tingling with life, interposed barriers to their departure, but they rode irresistibly toward the sea. The lynx saw them stranded in the shallows and clawed tentatively at them, different creatures, he found, than the larger fish coming upstream. The white eagle taloned them with a hiss. Easy to catch, he found, and tender. They came out of the great inland lakes, witnesses to the melting of mountain peaks and the flooding roar of the last of the snow water's escape.

The grilse had reached a strange estuary, strange and yet not strange. At this western shore he had passed through the estuary a year ago, himself a smolt then.

Smolt passed his nose and were gone. They poured outward, voracious now and toughened by their downstream movement, no longer insect hunters as they had been for the three years of their stream life. Now they pursued small fish and crustaceans and almost anything else they could catch; their appetites were near-insatiable. In their drop to the sea they had become more silvery, their movements more energetic. The sea would complete the transformation. Grow.

As they fell into the Gulf the first adults coming upstream passed them, ignored them. The journey upstream darkened the adults' bodies, lengthened their heads, and hooked their lower jaws into savage profiles; teeth grew in response to old race memories but now the salmon did not eat or need to defend themselves.

72

The grilse moved across the estuary and joined his comrades; a spasm of excitement passed through them. Haunted by that frenzied year at sea as smolts when they touched on distant sand bars and explored deep and gloomy trenches, they were ready to bring their sea experience to a magnificent climax. The blood of many grilse had splashed across ice floes and their scales had spun away in currents into the eastern hemisphere, their energy fiendish and their hunting voracious, as they had grown twenty to thirty times their original size in that year. They had come into this estuary with their spawning spirit brought precisely to maturity, yet inexplicably had left behind many hundreds of thousands of other grilse who lacked this spirit, this maturity, and who had chosen to remain at sea, comfortable and fat, and would take another year to make this journey. How they differed from the urgent grilse now in the estuary was a puzzle the sea kept hidden.

The grilse himself slid through the salt water, offering no answers; the Gulf was silent. Instead, it groaned softly at the turn of the season which now worked heat into all its joints and cast blanket rain against every coast.

The grilse gathered with his comrades, intent and feverish, at the head of the estuary. The moment was soon, and he felt it so strongly himself that it was as though he remembered every part of this place and where he must go. The moment—now?

No. The last of the pioneer adults must first work their cautious ways to the ends of their runs. They must

73

reach high into the cold hills or deep into the feature-less, scrubby pine and spruce lands of the northern shore. They must swim through the high red spruces of the west-ern shore and pass into tributaries of the main river. The smolts must finish their run out to sea. The estuaries and rivers must be left quiet and almost empty in the wake of all these salmon travelers.

Then the grilse could move.

IV

Midnight, and the moment had come. The grilse found himself impelled forward. He kicked his tail against the fish on either side of him, expelled the last of the brackish water in his body, and threw ahead into the fresh water. There, the same kind of elixir that had maddened the plankton—the water magic, clear, fast. Grilse crowded a channel, kicked up spray, competed with each other to be first ahead. The grilse might seem to know the river, but in truth he did not. He might seem to remember its every turn and meander, but a smolt has no true memory for such things. He might seem to understand how to handle the river, smash it into submission. No grilse would follow the slow example of his elders—circumvention and wily use of currents, rests in the lea of rocks, recuperation in deep pools. Instead, attack, die if necessary, but take the river. He urged himself into a strong funnel of current and his back broke water. For one electric second he was wholly in the air, then just as quickly down again. Water moved with fish, and cascades of bubbles lanced away from spillways over rocks to collisions with boulders. The grilse ran into a rock valley which shallowed sharply and thrust him back out of the water. Dead-end. He tried to jump, but flopped clear onto bare rocks. Panic. He flipped, fell, rolled back into the water, and let himself be carried down.

Movement up the river was a series of sharp collisions and enraged meetings. The grilse collected at the foot of a small waterfall and milled, indecisive for a second. Others piled in behind them and compressed them, and one grilse abruptly shot out of the water. The leap was abortive, intuitive, not aimed at the waterfall at all, but the percussive sound of his return to the water aroused others. From the writhing mass of fish, first one, then another jumped. These were calculated jumps, aimed at the waterfall, and the third one succeeded. Another success; the jumping became orgiastic. A score of fish lifted together, and the river seemed conquered.

The tempo of the river movement picked up, became metronomic in its insistence. No time for delay. The grilse filled a pool so quickly that the early arrivals were squeezed into the shallows by the latecomers. Barriers became higher, the leaps more sensational. The grilse found he needed to drive himself like a lance through shallow water and burst free explosively to see the weired water beneath, body bent like a flail with which to beat the air

75

and fly. The jump was as often as not misjudged, and his body jarred sickeningly on rocks as he fell. But one jump told him the height of the waterfall, the strength of the current, and the second took him over. He was possessed now, and after a jump he waited for nothing but fled on toward the mountains. Nothing mattered except to leap and hustle the shallows and leap again, and drive on and on.

At night the jumping became even more intense, and the sound of falling grilse bodies awoke the spruce woods and brought owls to watch at the water's edge. The grilse sought to break down the imperative of the land, to inflict himself on the living earth, and his energy and his grace enlarged the sound of the river and its echo in the woods. The trees, which had been pressing closer and closer against the river, caught and held the slap of his passing body.

Halfway up the river, a dozen falls, a score of low weirs, and three long rapids behind him, the grilse paused under the highest waterfall, which was fifteen feet high and dropped vertically. He paused and his comrades thickened around him, a thousand in the smoky water, then two thousand and more; this last waterfall was the final test which would determine the elite. He thrust his comrades aside and moved back, then made his run. The wind blew hard and the trees rushed by on either side, and he was out of the water and flying, a near-to-vertical leap which tossed him in the wind and twisted him sideways. He straightened his body convulsively and touched the curved

76

top of the waterfall. He would have been carried back but for his body curving again and firing him out and ahead into calm water. Behind, the moon caught the others seeking to follow and shone dilute wonder on their rising bodies and their midair collisions, on their failures and mighty falls, and asked what this supreme effort was worth. The salmon replied with their bodies, which hit the water so thickly that the sound of heavy applause rained on through the trees all night.

V

For those who made the last mighty leap the river was now a friend. When the grilse reached his place, known to him now, and stood guard near a rock, the Gulf was hardly a memory. Above him the robin stood and sang. The grilse was bruised, his magnificent physical condition left behind in the river. But he was now in a place where the process of wisdom would begin. He seemed to know that the river could be conquered, but its toll was high and subterfuge was needed to make the conquest sensible. His effort had been an imperial order from his species, and he, of this successful jumping commonwealth, had the privilege now of choosing how to ascend the river next time. He would not die; his mate would arrive soon and their milt and eggs would meet, and the smolts would be made here. But for the moment he waited, flanks pumping, and the river ran caressing water along his scarred sides.

The grilse could claim only an infinitesimal fraction of the total glory of the salmon, because the running had scarcely begun. Still in the Gulf was the main salmon contingent, perhaps thirty million fish who would come at the land in run after run through spring and summer and fall, each conditioned from different clock settings. They would fly past the ounaniche and the char and the trout, and run through white water and serene shallow with no backward glances at their Gulf home.

The grilse could claim reckless energy for himself. In his wake the rivers slowed. They filled with more salmon, then emptied from estuary upward. They filled again, and emptied. The pools stored salmon; wedge-shaped tails flicked and disappeared. The eagle's feet marked their backs, and cats raked them out of the shallows, and bears swiped them into higher leaps than they could survive. They flushed the rivers with eggs and milt and some of them died, and all the survivors finished exhausted, and fell down those proud waterfalls with a gasp of regret at the cost of their journey.

Grilse and adult fell together, and the grilse, when he reached the pungent salt water again and entered the estuary, was a memorial to his greatest spawning run. All the others would be anticlimactic. He had conquered the river and given his youth in sacrifice.

Chapter FIVE

I

The petrel danced her jig in the middle of an empty ocean
but her eyes were turned to the north. A mere thousand
miles separated her from the Gulf. Her cross-ocean flight
could not be interrupted by hunger, storm, or calamity.
She was locked onto an image of a remembered Gulf, cold
but compassionate and containing that single blessed island where she would make her most important landfall.
She flew quite directly and occasionally moved among
loose groups of other petrels, all of them headed north.
A great ocean stream rubbed against the colder waters
and threw up fluxes of plankton, and the petrel fed on

this. The sun sank into a saffron sea and the petrel danced into the twilight. She was early for her assignation with the Gulf; there was no hurry. The Gulf was not yet ready for her, although the seabird spring had already begun there, even before the last of the ice had disappeared. She spun on into the darkness, a speck of life adrift at sea.

Adrift? She knew where she was. All the petrels knew their places, eyes cocked up into night skies, eyes watching the sun, navigators so neat they could pinpoint one place in any sea and return to it again and again. The petrel would find her island, her burrow buried in the spruce, as she had done for a dozen years. A day-lover, she would nonetheless reach the island at night and circle it almost blind.

She flew north and zigzagged from one plankton nation to another, flew in magenta mornings, in drifting rain and sleet, flew when the sea was oily with the promise of changing weather, flew in dawnlight with a few hundred colleagues who represented several million petrels now converging toward Gulf waters, flew among shearwaters and saw a lone albatross swinging silently ahead of her. She flew as the first run of adult salmon reached their high river and stream places to spawn. She flew as the giant cod sank to the bottom after his herring feast and the lynx bedded himself in the forest, bloated with hare meat. She flew while the white eagle swung along the northern shore in search of the easiest salmon hunting, and one midmorning she reached her first destination, a staging place where countless seabirds gathered outside the southern strait. Turning in broad circles, she flew into serried fogbanks marshaled across her path and could hear the uproar of waters where current collided with current. She flew at leisure, butterfly wings touching the wings of others, and circled, awaiting the next step in the assault on the Gulf.

II

Before the seabird spring could begin the Gulf had to be cleared of the unwanted and the unnecessary; all those who had sought its indulgence at the death of winter. The demoralized dovekies, scattered about the Gulf in shocked memory of their wreck, gathered themselves together. They had been uncomfortable guests along the shores of the big island, and they must now seek territory in which to celebrate the next season. They moved offshore in gradually burgeoning flocks, tiny buzzing bees of the sea quite unlike the flittering petrels, and disappeared east into the mists of an arctic current.

The ivory gulls, scavengers in the wake of the seal invasion and hungry midwives at the whelping on ice, turned back toward the arctic and passed through the northern strait. The great glaucous gulls found the growth of spring uncomfortable and followed behind the ivories. Gyrfalcons who had contested the white eagle's domain along the northern shore abruptly abandoned the coast and flew north. The ptarmigans gathered, danced, then plunged with certainty into a northern snowstorm and disappeared into the arctic spring they knew must lie beyond. The snow buntings felt the pull of the arctic and were gone, and groups of longspurs traced thin lines into infinity.

The petrel danced on her wave and uttered a brief cry for her island. But the Gulf island was still too far distant, and did not respond.

Gulls cried out at the edge of the seabird spring of the Gulf, and were admitted. The herring gulls came drifting down western shore rivers, filtered along every coastline, jumped from island to island, prowled estuaries and beaches in their endless, scavenging way. Some came with the taste of the central continent on them, or with experience in hot southern seas or deep, cold inland lakes. They came into the Gulf in wild, upswinging flights and yodeled immediate demands for territory, for food, for meetings with their mates of the previous year, for instant satisfaction of their needs.

They spread out, reinforced from the south and west, and were joined by other gulls, the dainty kittiwakes who came from the east and from the north. Delicate as petrels, shaded the color of pale mist, they swept in through the fogs of the northern strait and planted themselves, in their fragile way, on every northern shore cliff that would accept their tiny nests.

III

The water dances of spawning fish had suggested ancient masques, and the seabirds of the Gulf spring now put them into precise forms. Their cries swelled and faded in the trough of every wave, echoed under every cliff, their ritual dances touched shore and island, cloud and ocean bottom. These singers, these dancers, were the toughest creatures on earth: bodies lean and muscular, accustomed to freeze and roast; bodies that could float or sink or tumble from great heights; bodies clumsy and bodies light as air. Few of them were beautiful, and there was little room in them for frivolous decoration or jestful excess. They were built into shapes and strengths suited to the sea, and that was all.

Dark-coated murres, sleekly streamlined in their tight-fitted suits, celebrated the spring in a black-and-white ceremony that banished the memory of so many months on the hard high seas. They had crossed no fortunate equators but had, instead, fought ice and gale and sleet and dense ocean snow. No circling subtropic seas for them, but rather an intimate and sometimes deadly liaison with the sea close under the arctic. No familiarity with the land for them either, but, instead, a strong hostility toward it. A quick rush into a shoreline bay to pirate food, and they were off again, a silent stream of intent black coats, to a place midway between the treacherous land and the point where the sea bottom dropped away to a distant abyss.

Opportunists, these murres, they flew for days with empty guts, and if they did not find upswellings of winter plankton where small fish were feeding they took to the deeps, dropping down two hundred feet into the darkest places of the herring winter. They would celebrate now, and it would be a paean to survival among southward-drifting ice pans, on great icebergs poised and turning, when gray visions of tomorrow were lost in horizon cloud and seabird cries broke in winds blowing west.

The celebration was about to begin, and the murres moved. Long before the petrel arrived at the southern strait the vanguard of murres wintering there had left. One hundred thousand of them poured through the strait into the Gulf and split, some heading up the island's west shore toward the northern strait, others turning south across the Gulf shallows. Behind them, another flight, and behind *them,* a third army of seekers. In a silent orchestration of spring, other flights turned east and then north into the face of the arctic current, picking up stragglers from refuge points near shore.

Puffins, relatives of the murres, remained offshore, and the petrel flitted among their silent commonwealths near the southern strait. They were spread wider than the murres and were more cautious. They sat drifting in great rafts, feeling the hostility of the shore and delaying the moment of landgoing as long as possible. They ignored the feckless petrels now flitting past them by the thousands, and concentrated instead on assuming their spring breeding costumes. Their summer beaks were growing, transforming narrow, pointed nebs into massive, wedge-shaped implements decorated white and red. Their eyes, plain all winter, became spectacled and took on expressions of comic intensity. When their spring plumage was complete and their colors shone bright, they took off in small groups, sped through the southern strait, and spread throughout the Gulf in search of the score of islands where they would breed.

IV

The petrel still waited, but impatiently. She anticipated a signal, as the grilse had anticipated his, and she would respond in the same way. She carried a detailed memory of her island. It was utterly undistinguished and sat squatly in a small and insignificant bay on the western shore. Its appeal was hidden. It had no special soil or atmosphere. Other islands within its view resembled it exactly, yet the petrel would ignore them, and so would all her comrades. On her first night visit there this year she would not be confused by the Gulf's voice whispering against other, identical islands. She would circle this one, and she would know it.

Almost without exception, the celebration points for

all the seabirds were islands. Islands catered to the individual needs of the various bird nations. Islands competed with each other to draw down puffins, proffering thick, easily excavated soil and clear, rolling grassland under which could be extended the tunnels that formed the puffin cities. Islands received puffins gratefully, willing to be drilled and counterdrilled. This year some, at the peak of their metropolitan triumph, would be abandoned to become ghost cities, honeycombed but empty, as the puffins moved on to greener islands.

Islands offered cliffs to the kittiwakes who could fasten a nest to a ledge of rock one inch wide. They offered broken ledges to gulls, who could wedge rough nests into cracks and crevices, and to murres, who needed six inches of bare rock ledge to hold their single eggs. Finally, they offered stepped cliffs to gannets and broad, high rock plateaus to cormorants.

The islands provided places in shallow waters where the interchange of life ran the gamut of herring and launce and capelin and cod and squid and swarming plankton throughout the seabird spring and summer. They provided the correct separation from the land— close enough to be among the teeming shore life, but distant enough to discourage a quick, risky swim by wolf or fox or other hunting animal with memories of seabird eggs and nestlings.

But the islands could not guarantee sanctuary from the winged enemies of the seabirds, and this the seabirds provided for themselves by coalescing into enormous, intimidating colonies. The white eagle had hovered high over these colonies, watched the swarming flights, heard the uproar of voices, and been defeated by the unity, by the vast, hostile collections of seabirds, individually helpless against him but collectively invulnerable.

V

The murres came out of the wispy morning mist, a thousand of them, and took up stations on a low slab of rock off the western shore of the big island. The rock looked incapable of supporting any life. It was a breeding platform, a moated fortress, almost inviolate.

A hundred murres appeared under the tall cliffs of a green island in the western Gulf, and floated, waiting. Six murres appeared at the edge of a forested island, lined with low yellow cliffs, on the northern shore. Murres poured through the northern strait and fanned out into the Gulf. Murres materialized out of clear horizons in thickening streams, and the Gulf felt two hundred thousand of them prickling its skin around a small island near the southern strait. A glossy black carpet of murres heaved, awaiting a signal, the arrival of their leader, some inspiration for the masses to begin their dancing, to conquer the islands and start the year's breeding.

A leader came; a leader came to all the murre islands, and he was always the same, anonymous, silent, commanding. He skulked inside the body of the straggling group of late arrivals or flew alone and low over the masses. No call was necessary. The birds on the water understood. They shook, and their inertia fled. The fringes of their carpets spread and thinned. Birds hurled themselves forward, upward, and the masses became joyful individuals. They decorated the sea with the marks of their dancing: great lazy figures, double-twirled, left in the wake of the hurrying birds; figures of eight dying in the smooth water.

The excitement was universal, transmitted from island to island all around the Gulf. The petrel felt it as late murres, responding to the pull of the dancing islands, roared toward the strait and disappeared into the Gulf. The excitement spread as hundreds of thousands of murres rose, wheeling, fluttering, hovering, into the sparkling air.

The sun, fresh-risen, burned away all mist, and the murres, like hummingbirds and hawks, hovered and dived, skimming the heads of the water dancers. The excitement was complete, uniting all the birds into a coherent unity. The excitement submerged, and the dancers dived and disappeared into deep green water in wild submarine chases.

The islands would be captured this day, the next, someday soon, when all the dancers were ready. In the meantime water dances and joy flights contained all. They gave courage, prompted daring, and birds sank toward their summer homes, knowing the rock and earth were dangerous. They tried to land, feet dangling, then roared away in panic at their temerity. But each day they grew bolder, until at last the granite and the gravel, the gully and the cliff were covered with birds, shoulder to shoulder, triumphant, the dancing done for this year.

The excitement of commandeering islands was shared by all the seabirds, although not expressed in the same ways. Lacking the ebullience of the murres, the puffins occupied their islands soberly. They were conservative, as indicated by their habit of tunneling rather than facing the summer boldly on naked rock, and their offshore dances were choreographed to less inspired tunes. They lined gray cliffs in red-and-white friezes, looked impassively down on their comrades floating underneath, looked up at solid, chunky puffins ramming overhead in graceless imitation of flight. Soon, *their* leader would arrive, and the year's digging would begin.

Islands of love and hate, islands that drew and repelled simultaneously. The seabirds must come to them, hate or not. The gulls tried to beat their islands into surrender by screaming at them from great heights; canopies of soaring, roaring birds helmeted every gull island. The islands remained silent, daring the gulls to land. The gulls were cowards at first, and refused all temptations, but grew bolder as the islands stayed mute. One bird, a leader, bolder than the rest, dared to touch his feet on island soil, screamed with delicious uncertainty at such bravado, and then landed. The other gulls responded to his challenge. Soon all the gull islands were occupied.

VI

The petrel held her wings high, frozen for a moment, listening. Had she heard the signal? The sea, muffled in the mist, whispered at her feet and the rustle of petrel wings mingled with the hum of plankton empire building. She listened, and this time heard the signal. The island called her very clearly, and she turned hastily, her waiting time now long enough. She was the last of the seabirds to respond to the Gulf spring, and she flew west.

This was no leisurely midocean journey; this was a swift flight to reality. She passed through the southern strait that night and reached the middle of the Gulf by morning. The island was within reach of her long, pointed wings. She was now with her friends, petrels on all sides, still spread wide but no longer circling and swinging back and forth. They thickened together and cut among low-flying ducks heading north until, near twilight, they turned and milled together. The island was close, and they were at the fringe of gull territory, almost within the grasp of land-based falcons. So they hesitated, and kept that safe distance until night dropped around them.

The run for the island was an individual act, unlike the communal conquests of the others. The petrel did not hesitate; she pushed forward blindly toward *her* island. Behind her, petrels tarried and settled on the water. Their signal was muted. Feeling neither restraint nor fear, the petrel drove on, and so precisely judged her flight that she reached the island exactly three hours after the fall of night. Nothing was visible. Thick mist muffled the sound of the sea. She could not see the other petrels but felt the presence of the island, warm, magnetic, reaching out for her, and like a great nocturnal butterfly she swept over it and sent down one joyful cry, six downfalling notes, and turned to listen for a response. The silent spruces said nothing. Back she came, and other cries stabbed around her, crystal notes in the gloom, and she called again, twisted in midair, and saw other petrels. The short night passed quickly. Her cries were stilled; she felt repulsed. The island would not accept her tonight, and she must be gone before the light caught her in this place and revealed her to her enemies. Before faint light came west she and her friends were gone from the island.

The petrels were correct in their suspicions of the island. The land was hostile, and they had been away from it for too long. But this did not stop them from returning every night. The petrel danced madly and filled the night above the island with interweaving cries that made the night sky shiver with sound and movement. Her cries penetrated the earth and reached her burrow and warmed the earth with their passion, and one night she crashed into low branches, fell to earth, and shrugged through a tiny entrance to her burrow, well and safely home from the sea.

Chapter SIX

I

Seabirds emplaced, the Gulf burst open, a supreme mix of colors gathering, polyglot and gay, of sounds dashing against cliffs and the hiss of water touching bony shores. The flower was open but needed visitors, witnesses to make sense of it in the hesitant sun, and migrants were marshaled.

The robin remembered the Gulf well now as he came north through wispy clouds. The track of the moon chilled a line from the wandering shoreline to the distant and invisible horizon, and his last arrival at the Gulf returned in sharp memory: the southern shore racing with drifting snow, catkins being tossed in the wind, the pines roaring, seabirds decorating offshore skies, and the waves shouting resistance to the prevalent east wind.

He remembered this time, when river highways filled, when birds were poised around him ready to surge north. It was a time of movement and excitement, involvement and change. The migrant flight shuttled north and drained the southlands and scooped up birds not of the sea: sparrows and warblers, thrushes and crows, cardinals and bluebirds, tanagers and redwings, killdeers, ducks, geese, mergansers, swans, vireos, phoebes, flycatchers, kingbirds. The Gulf was a flower, and the birds its pollinators.

The robin flew spasmodically, as befitted his mercurial character. He fled without regard for the wind, sleet, snow, and rain which inhibited many of the other migrants. He flew night or day, but clumsily at night, and dangerously so when the moon was down. He dropped among trees in a dusky bay, landed awkwardly in a dense hemlock, and went to sleep. He was alone. He awakened before dawn and flew immediately. Diverted for a moment by a mad collection of robins swarming to a small offshore island, he tarried there and dug worms and chased birds he would never know nor see again. Together they roared away for the mainland. Halfway across the gray water a peregrine falcon cut among them. The robin, old enough to remember falcons in his summer home, dropped to sea level and so escaped the falcon's charge. The drifting feathers of a dead robin hung over a wave.

He worked his way north, reckless by night and cautious by day. The territory was always unfamiliar. No memory of its details returned to him from other flights, even though the memory of the Gulf was strong.

The night flight was a machine of migration; the air sparkled with bright mechanical cries of creatures not in possession of will; sparrows inquired the nature of the night, and others answered. It did not matter how high or low the robin flew, he was always among migrants. He flew with them over dark, night-clouded forests; launched himself across stretches of open sea with them; heard them hit the slender tops of hemlocks which their day-eyes could not see at migrant speed. He heard them touch wave tops, and their cries faded swiftly behind in the midnight water.

Migration was fluid, living, dynamic, and nowhere more so than when wind or rain or snow sought to push it back, destroy it. The robin was well aloft this night, and found thick snow. He had outflown his comrades and, stimulated by his own audacity, he drove on overland. The snow pushed him down; his head crusted white with the stuff. The tips of dusky, forested ridges reached up and tried to pluck him out of the sky. He flew on, beyond the snow, and lakes shimmered in moonlight. Memory sharp in him now, he flew into the dawn, orange-hued at his right wing, flew on until he saw water ahead, water glowing in the dawn light, water stretching out of sight: the Gulf. Below him the southern coast, golden beaches, parklands concealing sleeping flowers and fruit, the familiar place. He settled, and became anonymous in a glade of welcoming pines.

II

At his place at the southern shore the robin paused, like the petrel, like the murres and grilse, for the signal that would send him to his summer territory. He waited while geese, baying at moons, faded north, and sparrows became thick, in all their varieties, dusky crowns gleaming, yellow patches sharp among gray: sparrows running helter-skelter through flushes of snow, sparrows suddenly gregarious at the tops of trees, sparrows of sand dune and grassland, sparrows of frost and barren, all of them collected for the moment at this shore of decision. The robin paused, and the sparrows washed around him. The Gulf let them escape; the robin heard their receding cries, and waited.

Some sparrows struck out immediately into the Gulf at night, knowing that land was within their reach somewhere in the darkness. Others, more cautious, swung northeast along the shore, jumping from headland to headland, pushing into upland country and resting at the fringes of mountain tarns glinting at the edge of winter ice. These sparrows reached the end of the peninsula, reached the end of the land, and paused to look across the southern strait. The big island, invisible in the mists of spring, offered no welcome; the sea hissed at them to turn back. They paused there, uncertain, until nightfall, and the petrel, silent as the mist itself, passed through the strait and into the Gulf.

Other sparrows, now at the robin's wing, swung west along the southern Gulf shore until, following the coast, they met more of their kind migrating inland. Their cries mingled, moved north at night, and drew others behind them into the unknown. As they flew, individuals dropped away to commandeer territories of the previous summer. They crossed wide stretches of sea and passed from fir to spruce to pine to tamarack, from bog to barren, from forest to rock mountain wall—sparrows triumphant in the blustering winds of spring.

III

Waves of robins reached the southern Gulf and surrounded the early robin; thousands of comrades strung along the long red shore. They shouted at the Gulf, and the petrel responded with a six-note cry, but the giant codfish was aloof to these absurd flying creatures. The grilse, in midair in his first great leap, was not yet ready to meet the robin. The white eagle drifted, so remote from robins it was as though they did not exist. One day the robins scattered. They exploded outward, carelessly cast at the Gulf. The robin found himself speeding along the coast in daylight. He cared nothing now except to reach his place. Behind him robins flew into the Gulf or turned up the curve of the coast into the mountains, flew into valleys and, night-blind, risked high winds at mountaintops before being swept out to sea on the wings of ecstasy. Thousands of them reached the southern strait and broke the crystal-cold air to allow following migrants passage to the island. They looked ahead. But this was no time to hesitate. They left the highland trees in darkness and plunged onward, crying to the water to support and save them. Beneath, the mute codfish swam, hungry.

At dawn robins reached the big island, hit a coast of barrenlands, and flew over lines of high cliffs marked with wedges of snow. They lofted above the cliffs and entered plateau country, an endless series of unwinding vistas of spruce and fir, aspens stiff in narrow valleys, and tall spires of family groups of white pines. This land unreeled, day and night; low mountains and long lakes, massive peaty barrens and white tumbling rivers. Robins dropped away or turned east into the mountains or swung along the south coast of the island to colonize the eastern shore, and only the hardiest of them reached the northern strait. The bones of an extinct forest stuck out of the bare ground. They paused, sobered, and the strait spoke to them. This was the end of the flight. They knew this, and slowly dispersed. One day, one night, sometime soon, a robin would cross the strait, but not now.

Meanwhile, in the western flight, the robin reached into tall uplands, mountains jagged against the western sky. He skirted the western shores of the Gulf and found shelter from belts of driving rain. The robins around him

97

were quieter now, sensing how close their moment of territory. No robin who took this flight could be driven out to sea. The wind, in fact, pressed them against the land. The robin laughed and a mountain leaped up five thousand feet. He laughed again at the mountain, and whisked up its slopes; the mountain smelled of the arctic; trees crouched, some dead; snow-girt rocks glowered in the cold sun. He remembered this place. Over the mountaintop and down toward a sheltering valley. Was this the place? It was kinder country. Sugar maple and beech and yellow birch flashed by, suddenly changing to tamarack and black ash. A compressed swamp passed beneath, and he cried out recognition. The sun at midpoint, he stopped on the banks of a small river and looked at his own reflection in a pool. There, exhausted and scarred, the grilse hovered. Both creatures met in this moment. The Gulf had ordered their presence here and, obedient to the end, they had come.

IV

The arrival of the landbirds beautified the forests and gave pulsebeats to the shores of the Gulf, already so well stirred by the mix of life rising inside it. The snipe, keen-winged, eager, fast, reached the southern shore and paused to shake late snow from their eyes, then left as soon as the moon

98

filled out and flew directly into the Gulf. They did not care to favor either shore, but took the Gulf at the center.

In twelve days they had conquered the Gulf, crossed the northern shore, and fled on. One-quarter of their number was held for three days by a storm at the tip of the eastern peninsula at the southern strait, and then they whisked forward into the big island. They split again there. Some flew due east until they reached the eastern shore and lowlands, dropping off occasional groups in valleys and lowlands along the coast. The others surged full speed up the western shore of the island and did not even notice the northern strait as they rushed on into subarctic haze.

Horned larks, shunning the high-flying night birds, skulked along beaches and river valleys and across barrenlands as they moved from the southern Gulf, where many had wintered, and passed up the eastern and western shores of the Gulf. They would drive into sand dunes and barrens and hardly feel the late blasts of winter along rocky northern shorelines. They would see cold-wrecked valleys where the snow bunting and the redpoll and the longspurs, visitors of a winter gone, had left their dead.

In three brilliantly clear and calm days, the skies of the southern Gulf opened up to the clattering, mechanical music made by great flocks of grackles. Suspicious, gregarious, they milled uncertainly, not knowing whether to turn east or west. They sought clear ground, preferably a gladed forest or lowland country recovering from a fire or other disaster. Their querulous flocks clacked out to sea, inspected offshore islands, and clacked back again, and there was much confusion as their prudence fought with their need to move, to search, to find.

The days closed, and late robins who had gone far south to escape the Gulf winter sped through the southern Gulf. Their tardiness was a penalty and sent them farther north into the territories of earlier robins, where contest and conflict followed. Behind them were red-winged black-birds, noisy as the grackles and as numerous. But they knew their place. They shunned the eastern peninsula. They knew there were no swamps or marshes up there, knew that this big island was too far north. They turned west and followed the coast in the wake of the robin. They reached into his territory after dropping half their number along the shore and inland. He saw them, in marshlands along the valley, perched on dead cattail stalks crying out their territorial rights. In ten days their females arrived, and their migration was completed.

It was spring, yes, but not too late for a blizzard; a heavy, wet, sticky fall of snow caught late-flying sparrows in its grip. The snow spread and mixed them up on the western shore, driving many of them past their places and dropping others on islands where they milled about in-decisively for a few days before crossing wide stretches of water in search of landmarks. They arrived back on the mainland in time to find cowbirds, who had skulked into the Gulf during the storm, waiting unobtrusively in val-leys for the bad weather to pass.

The migration was a month old, and the killdeers

100

arrived and spread into their territories along the fringes of marshes and on the western shore of the Gulf and in open parklands all the way along the southern shore, but not a single killdeer attempted to move up the peninsula toward the big island. The killdeers wrote a temporary pause to the migration. The south recovered its resources, marshaled its forces for another assault on the Gulf. The pause was taken up by some waterfowl, who collected on beaches and on inland ponds to consider the next move in their migration.

V

The robin settled into his place to the tumultuous tunes of the season and heard the dank forests echo with cries of despair, defeat, arrival, and discovery. He could now be an observer and see winter wrens appearing, no, materializing, as if they had been present all the time and had only just decided to show themselves. They passed and were gone to an offshore island, a distant cape. More sparrows appeared—was there no end to them?—and flew directly through a thin flail of snow into the valley and beyond, leaving colonist birds behind. Kinglets rode the swaying tops of great pines, flicked their wings, and disappeared. The robin wakened at night to the crash of the salmon and the grumbling of hungry bears and the night-pitched wailing of bobcats.

The Gulf's blood raced with life. Its body was suffused with landborne migrants, and expectant now of warblers, conservative and fragile migrants—or so it seemed—and one of the most numerous. Before they arrived the forestlands must be full awake and their insects abroad in tree-top feeding places.

The warblers also came in waves, their migration spread over forty days. The last of them would fly over Gulf birds bred and fledged there that year. But their migration was imperfect, with its insistence on flying close against winds of disaster. They flew at night on great broad fronts, almost regardless of weather, against strong diagonal land winds which pushed them offshore to confrontations with dawns in an empty sea. They flew on blindly and some, lucky, hit the big island when they had been aiming at the southern Gulf or its western shore. Others missed the island altogether, found themselves lost in oceanic fogs, and flew headlong to nowhere.

The warblers fetched up against lonely offshore rocks or tried to land on the backs of basking whales; they landed on beaches and sat on the sand, shivering, and were eaten there by fish crows. The warblers flew on, regardless, and what they lacked in technique they made up for in numbers. The grackles watched them with contempt from sheltered places, and when the mood suited them they stepped into the wind to join the crows in a warbler feast.

The warblers poured into the southern Gulf shore

102

and split, like those before them, and filled up the big island, and overflew the robin on their way north along the western shore. They crossed the northern strait and moved on toward the arctic. They flew with thrushes headed for austere highlands. They flew with vireos, who ignored all islands everywhere and favored the western route. They were still flying when the last stragglers of the migration, scattered flycatchers and the last of the sparrows, were closing the migration drama.

VI

The robin was mated, and his beak was full of mud from the riverbank. His mate, a bird from the shores of the southern Gulf, born the previous year, had not gone south. She had appeared a day after his arrival. He had fought two males for her and driven them down the valley. The grilse had gone. The chuckling river moved now with adult salmon. The valley smiled; catkins fell in the clouds; hills turned pallid green. The robin sang deep rich chords which hung in pollen-caressed air. He had met the migration and defeated it. He cared for nothing now except a rough structure of nest growing in low limbs of the tamarack, and he sang about this and about the clarity of the sun and the smell of the distant sea, and other things. His song harmonized and caught in its melody the mo-

103

ments of the other creatures of the Gulf, identically absorbed. The petrel was in her burrow, fertilized there by a night-born male who appeared like magic out of the black night; the lynx had mated in a slash of claws and caterwauling echoes in the forest's long twilight, and was hunting now with the other cat. The grilse, spent, was sunk in deep Gulf water. The giant cod moved with quick, certain energy through the southern strait. The lobster tugged at the sunken carcass of a dead haddock. Only the white eagle was denied the robin's song. Instead, he floated broad and slow in futile flight. Hawks and falcons passed under him. He slipped sideways across the sky to meet an eagle, but it was some strange creature not of his kind, and a male at that. He screamed his frustration, feeling this season in him so strongly that the absence of a mate enraged him. He called deep into the Gulf for her, but no one answered.

The eagle's reign at the Gulf was ending, his own migration in time nearly spent. He had seen the migration under him, life pushing to the limits of its survival in symbolic return to the arctic, but this evoked nothing for him except the absence of his mate. It was no reminder of the past, when the Gulf had been overlaid with ice much of the time and the southern Gulf shallows were mirror-smooth in the brief summer. Eagles had been common then. Pinnacles of ice had risen out of the water and beluga and walrus and narwhal had dashed across its surface. Snow geese had paraded overhead in search of open water, and larks and longspurs had sung in midair. The

104

Gulf shores had bloomed arctic poppies and purple sax-
ifrage then, the glaucous gulls had bred, and white polar
bears had moved smoothly from floe to floe.

The eagle was being made obsolete by the warming
Gulf. He waited, unable to change, and the Gulf slid away
under him.

Chapter SEVEN

I

The Gulf flowed fertile, its arteries enlarged with eggs. Eggs tinted the Gulf water milky white; eggs tumbled in streams and rivers; eggs whitened the tops of cliffs; eggs choked beaches; eggs flooded gravel and mud; eggs floated at the surface; eggs, eggs, eggs . . .

The petrel sat on her solitary white egg at the bottom of a deep burrow. The robin's mate sat on four blue eggs in the tamarack foliage. The lynx had fertilized his mate and four embryonic kittens curled in each other's limbs, lofted now with their mother in the low branches of a fir. The cod's eggs drifted up through six hundred feet of water, a million of them, reaching for the light of the surface. The grilse eggs were already hatched, and tiny smolts held places under riverbanks. The lobster's time was not yet come, but his moment of eggs was the more unusual for the wait. High above all the eggs, the white eagle hung, silent.

The Gulf was saturated with eggs. The eider ducks covered islands with blankets of their down and hid their eggs underneath. The gulls scratched out a patch of turf and each laid two eggs, exposed in the bare sun. Some eggs floated in the sea and others sank, while still others hovered midway between surface and bottom. Eggs were clamped to leaves, hidden in bark, buried in sand, dropped in mud, cemented to the bodies of their mothers. Eggs flew, floated, spun as free as birds. Each Gulf creature had a different notion of how eggs might survive. The petrel's solitary egg testified to her longevity despite the uncertainties of the open sea, while the twenty thousand eggs pouring out of the belly of the grilse's mate showed how few young salmon survived the sea run and return. The giant cod, hovering in the midst of an oceanic explosion of cod eggs rising snowlike to the surface, was lucky to be in deep water. Life at the surface, as the mortality of eggs was soon to demonstrate, was deadly dangerous. The lynx's four unborn kits would be long-lived, if they were lucky, but would remain vassal to the mercurial hare.

Within each egg were instructions concerning the exact moment when the herring might saturate the northern shore with spawn, when the lobster might move and

107

the petrel arrive; instructions concerning capelin assaults on the big island for years to come and the quality of cod life a century hence.

The eggs flowed and made the sea water milky under the eagle's wing. The herring gathered in a spawning ground well offshore, in deep water just inside the Gulf at the southern strait. Here, better than any other Gulf creatures, they expressed the irresistible message of the egg in the sea. This mothering stock fastened their eggs to the bottom, and the egg mass wound along the ocean floor with no break in it anywhere for more than a hundred miles.

The instructions in the eggs were irreversible, and held the progeny captive. The white eagle obeyed his orders and hung in the air, waiting. A mate would be arriving soon, he knew, and he must remain in place for her arrival. Then he would place his own sperm, as instructed.

II

It was spring, triumphant spring, and the egg fiesta danced on. It was spring, and the lampreys moved into the Gulf in the wake of the salmon, detached at last from Gulf-going fish and intent upon following the robin's example of building nests. They moved into a score of western shore rivers, branched out into hundreds of tributaries in search of fast-running water over gravel and stone bottoms. They used their sucker mouths to excavate nests, grip stones, and move them until nest hollows appeared. Each nest was flanked by a parapet of stones, and stream water eddied into them, refreshing the eggs cast there and swirling the milt among them. The lampreys turned their strange, jawless bodies toward the sea again and drifted past oncoming salmon who brushed them aside, drifted uncaring downstream, and died.

The lampreys died, but the sturgeon spawned to live on with a special kind of vigor. Their six-foot-long bodies cut through the Gulf toward river appointments. The petrel, flying in daylight toward the southern strait, swerved away from the sturgeons' great aerial leaps, which ended flat against the water and rattled the air with drumfire percussion. Such primitive creatures, so crudely energetic, so blindly set along inflexible passageways of time, were far from her own delicate adjustment to the Gulf. They swam at the tail end of millions of changeless years and possessed a stoic view of their function as animal dynasties rose and fell around them. Their kind had been present at the creation of the Gulf, and had fled from its destruction under ice. They had participated in its re-creation and had retreated from its second destruction. The rivers for which they were headed were created for them to conform to their stubbornly changeless habit. The southern shallows were their territory, drowned for them especially by a thawing arctic, created specifically for their leaping and cavorting at the beginning of their spawning run inland.

The sturgeons were the old ones, ancient river types who had no need to change. The petrel might become nocturnal to survive her island and the cod might break the ranks of his colleagues to find new opportunity, but the sturgeon went on blindly, two million eggs now maturing inside each female, and headed upriver for another rigid eon.

III

The robin's nest swung on the tamarack branch and four blue eggs rocked in its cradle. The robin came up from the river and looked down at the nest, wrenched awry, yolk still running from a single smashed egg left in it, and heard the sound of crow calls disappearing down the valley.

The robin's nest bunched down in the crotch of a maple, and four blue eggs showed their faces to the midday sun. The robin looked down and the eggs had gone.

Hermit thrushes built robin-sized nests in the western woodlands and sat, scarcely breathing, while night-running mice inspected them. Bluebirds squeezed into woodpecker holes at the southern shore and dropped four pallid eggs in the gloom. Orioles stitched basket nests to the highest swinging saplings and crossbills hid thickets of twigs in the highest branches of northern shore firs.

The robin flew into a grove of pines, quickly lofted high in their branches. He looked down; the eggs were still there.

Sparrows buried their nests in long grass and ran to them along concealed paths. Some warblers nested with them, but others, farther north, nested a hundred feet high. Swallows dived into banks along the southern shore, and two swallows nested in a creek bank in the big island's foothills. Vireos dropped four white eggs along the southern shore and cedar waxwings replied with clutches of gray-blue eggs strung along the northern shore. Kinglets took to the highest trees and few eyes saw the tiny, spherical nests which concealed their speckled eggs, while chickadees stuffed tree cavities with fur and feathers and laid down eight eggs.

The eggs poured forth. The robin, venturing through a swamp to the valley, was chivvied by redwings who guarded eggs among marsh reeds. Farther down the valley he passed an uproarious tree where a hundred grackles clustered, clattering mad language to each other, and he hurried by, already witness to hawks being chased away from the tree.

The eggs of spring were spread around the Gulf like white sand grains flung carelessly from a cloud. They settled evenly everywhere—in marsh and grass, in tree and bush, in hollow and hole, in frail refuges on bark, buried in tunnels. The robin flew free among them and heard the thrush's query and the goldfinch's caress, and celebrated the hatching of his mate's third clutch of eggs by fluting a short and private song in deep woodland.

The eggs of the land spread thin and wide and even, but the seabirds would have none of that. To them the land was unfriendly, and they compressed the essence of the sea into one concentrated space. They pushed their eggs together and held them there with an hysteria which drove off eagles.

The murres settled their islands in black angry masses which roared a challenge to the sky. Their eggs flushed out of them and fell in green slime or rolled into rotting puddles. Murres collected on cliff ledges that were exactly the correct width to receive them. Their eggs were tapered to roll elliptically, just short of falling over the edge. Ten million murre eggs were contributed to the Gulf in thirty days, and were gratefully received.

In their soft islands, the puffins showed their lack of humor as they dug and dug at the soil to make safe havens for solitary white eggs, half a million laid down on this island, a million on that island, fifty on this low patch of turf among the cloudberries off the big island, a thousand in a low bank at the bottom of a cliff made joyful by kitti-wakes.

The petrel sat on her single egg and the earth moved around her. New burrows were dug at night with frail, short bills and clawed paddle feet, and eggs poured into the earth of the island by the hundreds of thousands. She sat without pause for four days and nights, and each night brought her the sweeping cries of multitudes of petrels returned to the island from sea hunting. On the fifth night she heard her mate's voice among the multitude, heard him land outside the burrow, shuffle forward and then, with a flirt of his wings, plunge into the burrow beside her. Together, they gurgled and cooed a delicious song over the possession of their solitary egg. Shortly before dawn she left her mate in the burrow and fled from the dark island. Other petrels flew silently around her until, at dawn she was well away into the Gulf and free from the island, free to hunt.

The eggs poured out: gull eggs in rough tree nests, in shallow caves, among shoreline rocks, in great island colonies numbering thousands, and solitary eggs on sharp-etched headlands; guillemot and razorbill eggs thrust carelessly into shoreline rocks yet well protected from everything except the blurring run of falcons, who often left the eggs orphaned; eggs in cup-shaped nests fastened to narrow ledges by the dainty kittiwakes, line upon line of them decorating cliff faces; eggs laid singly in built-up piles of rubbish that the gannets called nests; eggs falling free from cliffs at every alarm; eggs guarded by cormorants on bare rock homes; eggs whose birth was the supreme test of mortality and whose survival was the measure of its quality.

IV

The lobster moved majestically from his refuge, tiptoes barely touching the sand, and minced forward into a faint bottom current. His blood, finally, had been stirred by something other than the search for food and shelter, and he moved steadily to the fringes of his territory, a rough demarcation of black rocks strung across the sand and disappearing into the gloomy water. On the other side of that line another lobster held domain. He dared not cross the boundary without a fight, yet his mission lay beyond that territory. He stood high, his swimmerets moving rapidly.

The lobster, slow-processed, remained snug behind his armor while the other fortress people moved into prominence throughout the Gulf. The shellfish of the shore now twisted through ancient dances of desire, all in slow motion. The whelks, in whorled, snail-like shells, massed wherever there was shellfish hunting in the tidal shallows along the western and southern shores of the Gulf. They congregated particularly in the bays and river estuaries, and in this spawning movement offered a series of enigmatic egg collars which would, in the next thirty days, litter the shores at low tide with swirls of gelatinous stuff enclosing the eggs. The collars were decorative, symmetric,

114

even artistic.

The spawning of the whelks began at the full moon, with the water low in an estuary west of the southern shallows, and reached a climax when the tide was low just before dawn or just after sunset. The wide tidal flats south of the shallows were wreathed with mist and sounded to the hollow cries of invisible shorebirds. Kelp sprawled at the fringe of rock and sand pools, and gulls hovered, accusatory eyes in midspace, awaiting one chance at the unwary, one sign of a shell not quite buried, one track of a shellfish foot left too recently after the fall of the tide. In a brief hour before darkness, the water chuckling at its lowest point, a few of the whelks were weeded out of the spawning legions as they attempted to spawn in too-shallow water. Gulls plummeted and broke into the sea, and the whelks flew briefly before being dropped and smashed on rocks. Totally absorbed in the obsession of the moment, the whelks were insensitive. Falling to death from the beaks of gulls, they felt nothing. They still attempted to continue spawning, clear mucsin coming slowly from their feet, oozing on through shattering collisions on the rocks.

Most of the whelks, however, spawned in the deeper shallows, just below the gulls' vision. Each shellfish turned on its side and pushed out a long, plump foot. These uncaught whelks extruded the mucsin into the shallow water. It waved, bannerlike, in the slow-moving water.

The tide turned; the whelks suddenly became active. They burrowed into the sand. The water passed over them,

115

deepened, and they pushed down three or four times their lengths and turned once again on their sides, their shell spires pointed toward the surface, making ready for collar molding. Each creature began circling in the sand, always clockwise, extruding the sand-collar jelly and, in turning, thrust the shell against the collar, pushing it against the sand, shaping it. The movement of the shells ground sand into the collars, and as more jelly material was extruded during the circling the collars were built up in thickness and strength. Buried in this material were the egg capsules. Finally, still working deep under the sand, the whelks circled again, applying another layer of jelly while simultaneously nudging the almost-finished collars up to the surface. With the sand collars finally exposed, the whelks turned and disappeared deep into the sand. The collars remained along shorelines like insensible monuments.

Spawning rippled substance through the Gulf tides and the energies of currents and whirlpools. Every wave contained testaments to spawning as larval millions wriggled and the plankton spun onward. The oyster nations joined the ritual. A new temperature reached and held them, a hormone spilled by oyster males flushed the water; one hour after dawn spawning began, and continued without rest until all the females were empty of eggs. The male oysters opened their shells slightly and let out streams of sperm—sea smoke, really—and it fell on females whose shells were still shut. They roused, opened their shells slowly, and clapped them slowly. Eggs spilled with each

116

clap. Thus began a game of chance. Each male sperm swam blindly in search of an egg and had to bump into it to fertilize it. Without that collision, billions of eggs died within the day and fell to the bottom, where the bottom dwellers ate them.

And now, the slow-moving lobster, deliberate green fortress, acted. He knew, finally, that the boundaries of territory were no longer relevant, knew that he must move through them in search of a female. She must be a female made helpless by recent molting, unable to resist his sexual advances, passive while he inserted sperm into her container. Afterward he would back off, eye stalks rigid, and return to his territory. All male lobsters in the Gulf moved. Their archaic sex act, unlikely in its extreme conservatism and deliberation, was so successful it did not need to be changed. The sperm was placed, but it remained remote from the act of egg laying.

The females first began egg laying in the southern shallows within the feel of the shore, in shallowish, stony-bottomed strands. They were old-shell lobsters who had changed their shells the previous summer and had been impregnated then. They were imbued, like the seals, with a moment almost twelve months old. They rolled on their backs in a gesture of slow and graceful abandon, claws flung back wide in a surrender they had not offered the previous year, legs akimbo, the front parts of their bodies lifted, the fan end of their tails slowly covering the vulnerable, unarmored underbody of the tail.

Eggs appeared through two small openings at the roots

117

of their second pair of walking legs. Slowly they flowed down, six to eight abreast, until they reached the pocket formed by the folded tail. Each egg was round, dark green, glistening. The eggs fastened themselves unerringly to one of the five pairs of swimmerets, but not before they passed the sperm sac between the last two pairs of walking legs. The sperm waited there, fresh and alive, as though deposited yesterday instead of the previous year. The fertile eggs would stick in place while they matured and grew perfect infant lobsters inside them.

The lobster passed on through the territories of many others and heard the crunch and grind of lobsters caught and eaten while molting. He traveled only at night and so escaped the lobster hunters, knowing that soon he would find a female and place his seed.

V

At the moment of spawning, each creature hinted at the complex history of its kind. The diatoms divided and died, and that seemed simple, but now the copepods danced a mating minuet so delicate it diminished what had seemed graceful in other creatures. The male copepods, invisible to a bird's eye, manufactured tubular-necked vessels into which they squirted sperm. Then a hundred thousand square miles of the Gulf water shook as the male copepods advanced, each one carrying his container, his bottle, and swimming in search of a female. It was a blind and thrusting search aimed not at individual females but at the generic notion of females. When they were found, the females received the bottles, placed to their abdomens with infinite care and accuracy by the males' limbs. The charged bottles supplied sperm for passage into storage receptacles in the bodies of the females. From there the sperm were conducted into the females' ovaries and fertilized the eggs singly as they passed outward into the Gulf.

Hydroids, which look like plants—waving ferns, miniature trees, tiny branches—but are actually colonies of animals knit together in a cooperative search for food, thronged the shallowest parts of the southern Gulf, and now they grew a new generation of creatures which budded on the branches of their bodies. These children remained captives of their parents, but they in turn took reproduction a step further and formed yet another generation of free-swimming medusae which swam off in search of new opportunity.

The medusae rose in billions, became carnivorous, ate the copepods, and matured quickly. Soon they laid eggs and spread sperm, and this third generation sank to the bottom to find places among the rocks of the shore and in the shallows. There they began the reproductive cycle anew and lived as hydroids, which looked like plants. It was as though freedom had failed, and they must now experiment again with captivity.

119

VI

The giant cod moved rapidly. His hunger gripped him. He knew exactly where he must go and what he must do. The new season of the Gulf offered him the greatest hunting he would know this year, and he must use the spawning moment to gorge. But he was only one player in the spawn-hunt drama; throughout the Gulf other creatures followed the spawners, seized the day.

Flounder lay stupefied on the bottom, sated on herring eggs eaten along the western shore and in the shallows near the southern strait and at a dozen places around the big island. Seals who were resident Gulf animals knew how vulnerable the flounder were and came down and snapped them up easily. Herring spawn stuck to northern Gulf rocks, so shallowly placed that it appeared above water as the tide fell. The feast of eggs was too good to miss. Scores of ducks came down out of the racing skies to fuel themselves out of the Gulf and into the arctic on these herring eggs.

But the banquets were not without incident. The white eagle, hung high, saw the ducks converging and watched while they fed. Then, remembering a previous year at this place, he planed down slowly to bring the ducks into large focus. Gabbling and gobbling with gluttony, the ducks showed the eagle their oblivious shoulders, and he, half wary, plucked a drake from their mass and flew downshore with his screaming victim. The ducks scarcely paused. A few leaped into the air, but most concentrated on the food and let the eagle go without reproof.

The capelin were spawned at the central Gulf plateau. These myriad, silvery, herringlike fish, the second greatest middle nation in the Gulf, had selected a broad, sandy bottom on which to lay down their eggs. The giant cod had knowledge of the time and place of their work. He moved swiftly toward them, but he was beaten to the feast by millions of creatures who had preceded him. Herds of haddock had already gathered. They intermingled with the tiny, hurrying fish around them and in places were buried in the hordes of familiar fish. The capelin, leaping, trembling, unheeding, went through their tiny ritual, eggs pushed into the sand, milt spurting, while the haddocks, dark-backed leviathans by comparison, moved solidly forward and pushed the capelin aside as they snuffled the sand like grazing cattle and gulped down crops of eggs.

When the giant cod reached the spawning grounds capelin were reeling away, spent, and he cut through them; soon his stomach bulged and jerked with a score of living fish in it before they died, and he was sated. Other cod appeared, and the capelin hordes lost cohesion and scattered too wide for easy hunting. The giant cod turned east toward the shores of the big island.

Eggs filled the water, the air, the forest, every pool and swirl of current, every beach and rocky shoreline.

121

The capelin of the eastern Gulf must spawn on coastal sandy beaches. The codfish knew this. The gulls knew it, and so did the shearwaters, those hemispheric travelers who remembered the capelin even when they were thousands of miles away from the Gulf. The resident Gulf seals knew the capelin, as did the pilot whales and the squid and many others. The capelin were tragic figures in the Gulf, doomed to enact a national disaster in order to reach beyond the spawning.

The cod found himself swimming in long, uphill flight with capelin thinly interspersed around him. Other cod swam with him. Finally all were at the surface, and the land was visible a few miles distant. Here the capelin must draw themselves up in a series of divisions to attack the shore frontally and separately, like waves of people flung at a target. In forming their troops they stoically endured the cod and his friends, who ripped them to pieces. The cod was so possessed as he swam below the capelin that he fired himself upward at the dark bodies reflected against the surface and frequently leaped clear out of the water. The capelin endured the falling gulls and re-formed around seals so bloated they lay on their backs, bellies bulging, half asleep. They endured vanguard squid, which attacked en masse and shredded divisions of them.

The turmoil of the offshore attacks meant nothing to the capelin. Only the egg was important, only that distant beach had relevance. They formed, re-formed, died, milled, and awaited a signal to send them ashore. And it came, predictably just before dusk, and they charged the shore.

122

The cod moved in with them. The capelin ran in a series of frontal assaults, one following the other in precision lines. Each female was held between two males, and they hit the beaches together, rolled in the murmuring surf, and eggs and milt spilled out simultaneously.

The spawning was an act of excess, there being no apparent connection between the capacity of the beach to accept such a quantity of eggs and the desire of the fish to find a suitable place to spawn. All they knew was that the time was right; advance they must.

The waves of fish came in monotonously all during the twilight, long after the cod had retired offshore, so bloated he could hardly swim, scraps of capelin flesh escaping from his jaws. The capelin passed him relentlessly, division upon division, and a freshened wind pushed up bigger waves on the beach, each containing its load of wriggling fish. The tide turned in the early evening and the wind continued rising. Now the fish were stranded, and the act was changed from debauch to debacle.

In the morning, the beaches were a shambles. Glistening eggs, far too high on the beach ever to hatch, settled into dense masses. Offshore, screaming gulls and shearwaters, leaping codfish and darting squid, whales and seals harried the capelin back into deeper water and left them poorer in numbers, but no wiser.

VII

The cod's time had come, yet what had taken him away from the shore and sent him down in a long plane to the bottom? What had brought him to this meeting with a population of codfish just about to spawn? He was neither their age nor size. But he would supply milt, and that was all that was asked of him. He was part of many similar gatherings at many places in the Gulf. Some fish collected in seven hundred feet of water, others in less than two hundred. The eggs flooded, the milt gathered in clouds, and the cod nations sent capsules of life on first journeys. The eggs drifted slowly upward through conflicting currents, through interposing cold layers of water, until they bloomed at the sun-warmed surface. Each egg would soon contain a perfect, fully developed young cod, black eyeballs bulging and tail curled around the sphere and tucked under his chin. Then the eggs would join currents which would take them to where they could drop safely to the bottom and begin lives as adults. The giant cod, in response to his hunger, was already speeding to new hunting grounds.

The cod spawned into currents which carried their eggs to places of hatching and some chance of survival. But haddock, clustered on the central Gulf plateau, seemed less well placed in their firmament. They spawned now, like the cod, at depth. Their eggs drifted up and floated in the same way, at the dictate of circular currents which swirled like giant eddies in the center of the Gulf. But this year the traditional, the accustomed, the commonplace became a rare disaster. The outflow of haddock eggs was customarily prodigious, but the blind eggs knew nothing of cosmic alteration in the sea itself, changes originating in the arctic and transmitted to the Gulf with lethal delayed reaction. Heavy snow and a fast and savage thaw had sent arctic water pouring south, and this water, plunging through the northern strait into the Gulf, had malformed the central eddying. The haddock could not sense the difference between a current running at a mile an hour and one running at a mile and a half. But the difference was critical.

The haddock eggs drifted south, as they had always done. They reached the edge of the plateau, as they had always done, where young haddock should fall into shallow slope waters. Now the eggs drifted on. For five days they were pushed south under a warm sun and were then ready to hatch. But instead of three hundred feet of water under them, instead of plateau shallows for the beginning of larval lives, they were now over deep water.

They sounded, and began a journey one mile down.

VIII

In the end, the parade of eggs was overwhelming, too many to be counted, too many different habits to make sense. The bottom-feeding flatfish, the sometimes enormous halibut who spawned soon after the cod, did not send their eggs to the surface nor did they stick them to the bottom. Instead they directed them, by the remotest kind of control, to the middle depths. The eggs were heavier than surface water, but lighter than the deeper water. They floated in the middle depths, and the creatures who might have loved halibut eggs hunted above and below them. Some shrimp spawned and sent their eggs to the surface and then inshore. Others spawned in the deeps and the eggs remained down until they hatched. Eggs rose and fell, larvae sank and drifted, and at last the Gulf, surfeited, ordered all egg laying in its waters to cease. The order was imperfectly understood, and eggs still flowed whenever quick chance came.

On land some lives had not even begun to think of eggs. Instead they offered a parade of subtle colors as evidence that not all re-creation need be in terms of raw energy and stupefying numbers. The forests would not cast seeds for many months, or years. Instead they offered flowers. All along the south shore the red pines of the

126

southern Gulf flowered—male flowers dark purple, female flowers scarlet. The jackpines, sweeping up the southern end of the western shore, flowered their males yellow and their females dark purple, which seemed to contradict the red pines' careful message concerning their males, and the puzzle was compounded by the tamaracks, with their yellow male flowers and red female flowers.

The tree flowers were tiny jewels in boundless forests, their sparkle lost in a sea of trees. The white spruces flanking the western rivers showed pale red male flowers which would soon turn yellow, and the female flowers—red on this tree, but yellow-green on the next—illustrated the puzzle of evolution. Who saw the difference between one flower and another? Perhaps it was the flowers themselves, watching each other.

The colors marched away out of sight, the dark red male flowers of the black spruces, roots deep in sphagnum bogs, and the female flowers accompanying them in sympathy. The hemlocks were bold with yellow male flowers and pale green females, and the balsam fir matched them with yellow males, but their purple females were closer in color to the red pine males or the jackpine females.

The Gulf had no need to explain these contradictions as it drew an enormous breath at the end of spring. The season of the Gulf looked good, peaceful, plentiful. It promised warmth along with humidity. It promised prevailing winds, therefore predictable times, and for this all creatures might be thankful in the summer of the Gulf.

Chapter EIGHT

I

The Gulf stored its eggs and held them until they hatched. Its youngsters renewed and restored and remade the Gulf, but the hatching of the eggs often seemed less birth than sacrifice. To survive, and to keep its sinews lean and strong, the Gulf was witness to the deaths of most of the youngsters. But then death—quick, bright, forgettable— was no tragedy. The dead passed on and, in the manner of their dying, educated the survivors.

The giant codfish was no accidental survivor. He lived by flexible criteria which often put him beyond the obedience principle of the Gulf. His cross-Gulf flights, sometimes a thousand miles at a time, were instantaneous responses to stress. He repealed all Gulf laws when necessary and obeyed his individual authority. Thus while his less flexible contemporaries starved, he found food.

The robin was no accidental survivor either. He was first to see the hawk—a small enough perception—but he was also quick to realize that a nest could be built too low or a migrant flight be made too high in a gale. He had a fraction of extra wariness that stopped him from standing naked in a splash of sun and turned him more quickly from his reaching enemies.

The petrel, long-lived anyway, played out her life with different emphases. Her personality was less important to her survival than the nature of her nationality. Her kind had learned to regulate their numbers with single eggs laid on the far side of the petrel hemisphere. The petrels matured with meticulous lack of haste, and so adjusted their numbers to balance with the plankton populations.

The creatures of the Gulf were obedient in their individual ways. The eagle had no enemies, He might reach his full life span and extend it toward eternity through his youngsters were he not caught in an ironic play where the Gulf deprived him of the one thing he must have to survive. He waited, tight as a green sapling, for the Gulf to change its mind.

Pushing through long nights of alien country, the inexperienced grilse entered his most dangerous age. He had no reservoir of knowledge to guide him safely to the edge of the arctic, no previous cognizance of a distant gathering of salmon where a twenty-thousand-year-old ritual meeting place called for his attendance. The sea bottom was as dark as moonless midnight, falling here to a mile in depth, rising there to a sunken mountain range rifted with valleys and foothills, scoured by currents and sectioned off by different temperature layers along which he might move comfortably, like a robin in a warm wind, toward his destination. But no matter how far he traveled he remained a vassal of the Gulf, a prisoner of his river so long as he lived.

The lynx was no longer hungry, but he was equally helpless in the hands of the Gulf. He watched the upsurge of hares, saw their progeny leap carelessly under his nose, and reached out a languid paw, and killed. The Gulf rewarded him for his stoic winter hunger, applauded his burrowful of kittens, and would, perhaps, delay its punishment of the young lynx until he became old and his persecution of hares less vigorous.

The lobster remembered nothing, offered nothing, and, in his eighth year of life, looked into gloom now becoming less dangerous by the month as he outgrew the jaws of predators.

Summer began, and the obedient creatures produced the climaxes and disasters which provided a microcosmic view of the future of the Gulf.

II

A few hours after milky clouds of sperm settled among the oyster colonies of the Gulf's southern shallows, hatching began. The uncountable larvae were propelled by tiny moving hairs on their bodies. These vibrating cilia were favorite propellants among the small and the meek. The cilia turned the creatures in the water, pushed them up a little, down a touch, but could not move them very far. Most of them, in the southern shallows at least, had very small distances to travel, since the currents were weak.

But at the eastern end of the shallows an offshore arm of the active outflow, mellowed by conflict with other waters, passed through. For tens of thousands of years it had scooped up all the oyster larvae shed there and taken them on a voyage into new territory. Each voyage covered a precise distance; each terminated at the end of twenty-one days when the larvae sounded and dropped to the bottom. This group of voyaging oysters, along with all the comrades they had left behind them in the other oyster colonies, developed two tiny, beautiful shells within a day and a half of fertilization. They resembled clams one-three-hundredths of an inch long. Their rudimentary propulsion—the cilia—was used to push them to the bottom when they were in danger of being driven ashore in

131

heavy coastal seas.

The oyster voyagers swung south, toward the southern shore, then east as the current felt the warping effect of the shore. They passed within sight of low red hills where young songbirds, just hatched themselves, flailed stubby, unfeathered wings. The larvae swung northeast and the coast was transformed into tall rock cliffs with towering flights of gulls and other seabirds. After four days of travel the young oysters were pale red. They had moved nearly fifty miles from their place of birth. At ten days the oysters turned dark brown. A hundred miles from their place of birth the coastline flattened into a long series of hogsbacks plunging sharp, angry rivers into the sea.

The hills diminished; mist flooded the horizon from a point where another, cooler current collided with the oysters' vehicle. The larvae swung almost due east as the current warped away obediently from the new current and passed under cliffs where migrants to the big island waited to cross the southern strait. At fifteen days from their place of birth the young oysters were almost ready to find permanent homes. They had traveled more than a hundred and fifty miles and were nearing the limits of current travel.

At twenty-one days their voyage ended. Their new home seemed ideal; the bottom was shallow, quite warm, and offered refuge. Close inshore, beds of marine grasses waved. In deeper water lay the empty shells of a long-extinct scallop colony. The oysters sank, each now visible

—the size of a grain of pepper—and with the ability to see through its own eyes. Each was equipped with a foot which projected from between the two shells and could drag the young oyster in search of a new home.

Down came these specks of life over hundreds of square miles of new territory. The ritual of the search was exhaustive. It was the one opportunity they had to choose a place to live—the place where they would breed, if they were lucky, and eventually die. They swam vigorously as they came down, in anticipation of the search. They reached the solid floor of the sea, with its jutting rocks and boulders and its strata running for miles into deep water.

Each young oyster sought a slime-free place, a good hard place, where others of its kind had already settled. Some larvae settled on a walrus tusk, but rejected its slimy coating and swam off. A long outcrop of rock was attractive, and millions settled there, swinging immediately into a ceremonial dance, circling until they were satisfied. Then each tiny creature lay down on its left side and extruded a blob of cement which flowed down between shell and rock. Within minutes, the oysters were fastened.

The sounding of the oyster larvae was a triumph of travel. Few other marine Gulf creatures went so far as these youngsters. It was an epic voyage, but a waste of time since the sounding area was fatally faulted. In early winter another arctic current, unmodified, reached into this oyster haven; it was traditional. It swept over the oyster host as it had done for thousands of years. The

133

youngsters would survive for a while, thirty days or so, and then they would die, as they always did here. Within a month there would be no trace of the legionary creatures who had settled there.

The children of the sea prospered and they died. They traveled in a Gulf whose arteries and veins led to a coldly beating heart. The oyster voyagers were destined to die, and so were their comrades left behind in the southern shallows. These young oysters faced a different death. Starfish, who coveted oyster flesh, also occupied the shallows. They anticipated the oyster spawning by thirty days, and the young starfish were hatched and free-swimming and well spread throughout the shallows when the young oysters fell. As they dropped into their new home the starfish ate them. They would eat little else except oysters for the rest of their lives. One day the surviving oysters might exceed them in size, but they would never have enough strength to resist the starfish's relentless, multiarmed pull against their shells, a pull that might last for half a day.

The oyster legions drifted on, testing and retesting the cold heart of the Gulf. Indefatigable, they sought to break down the Gulf and make it yield to their wishes. For nearly twelve thousand years a nation of oysters spawning along the northern edge of the Gulf's southern shallows had liberated their eggs very late in spring, after the prevailing winds had altered current flows. Their eggs drifted to the center of the Gulf, over the deep trench where the redfish lurked, and sounded within view of the southwestern shore of the big island. They dropped into what appeared to be a thriving population of oysters, but an odd group, this. They lived there, yet they never spawned. The water never became quite warm enough to trigger the hormone signal; no flow of sperm came from the males, no stream of eggs issued from the females. The colony was a eunuch community perpetuated by absent parents who sent their children, perpetuated with a sense of patient failure that eventually, as the Gulf understood, would triumph when a slight warming of the water occurred. Then the oysters of this place would breed; then their progeny would sweep around the big island and colonize its shores.

III

The giant cod traveled swiftly. He had anticipated herring at the edge of the submarine shelf, but they had not come. A colony of scallops, once thriving on nearby rock ledges, had disappeared. He pushed forward, impelled by his hunger, and his body consumed itself to fuel his flight. North, near a shallow island shore, a population of young cod often grazed, and he headed for them. Above him, beside him, other cod cast out their progeny in a series of grand gestures that put hatching cod eggs into every mouthful of water.

135

The cod on the northern shores of the big island sent their eggs up into the arctic-drifting water, which took them south to a meeting with a warm midocean current. They would die in this meeting of warmth if they did not hatch within thirty-five days. Farther offshore other great cod herds hunting in deep water cast their eggs into the coldest surface water where they would not hatch for forty-five days, but this delay in hatching dropped them exactly over an oceanic plateau where they replenished a nation of cod living there.

The helpless eggs hatched, and remained helpless— tiny codlings attached to sustaining egg yolks floated upward. The time of hatching was critical. The young cod must keep the company of plankton, which they ate as soon as they developed mouths. But the plankton was growing too. The first billions of codlings to hatch in the central Gulf ate well, but after thirty days new arrivals faced an odd paradox: as their mouths developed they found the plankton grown too big for them to catch, and so they died of starvation amid plenty.

The Gulf distributed death but it also offered special variations on the theme of survival, and so kept numbers stable. The haddock nation whose eggs had been sent drifting so confidently beyond the southern strait had made a vain gesture. The eggs hatched and the young haddock went down into nearly six thousand feet of water. All were dead from starvation before they reached the bottom. But although this nation would be missing a generation of its kind, another haddock group collected along ledges west

136

of the big island and there felt the delayed impact of the early arctic thaw. Their eggs filtered three hundred miles down the coast and found an ideal, haddockless territory. A new nation would prosper there for a decade until it died out from senescence or was again accidentally replenished by an early thaw.

IV

The Gulf's children hatched hot and quick and warmed the air with their jostling numbers. But the young lobsters were cool. They had waited in slow-maturing gestation under their mothers' tails for nearly twelve months until this moment of hatching. Swamped at first in dark green yolk, they used up the yolk to grow form and then content, and the tension between the two was perfect. The eggs lengthened and lightened in color as they matured. They were ready to hatch now. The underside of any egg-bearing lobster showed masses of tiny eggs, up to seventy thousand in a large female, and each egg glistened with the dark beady eyes of the watching but unhatched baby lobster.

The young lobsters were born soon after the impregnation of the fertile females was ended and the egg-laying females had forced out the last of the oozing streams of life which dropped into the pockets of their tails to await hatching. Then the egg-hatching females stood erect, on tiptoe, and faced into the current, claws thrust straight ahead and tails raised high, creating graceful inverted parabolas.

Egg cases ruptured; the young lobsters were ready to leave, but they lacked the final incentive. The females provided it. They shook their swimmerets violently, creating rapid currents. The young lobsters pushed free and clouded the water with tiny reddish specks that hardly resembled lobsters at all. They headed for the surface, where they would eventually molt three times on their way to a fourth stage of transformation. Then they would resemble their parents.

The release of young lobsters in the southern Gulf shallows was not far short of the immense oyster spawning. Six hundred billion lobsters swarmed upward in the southern shallows, where they joined the slow counterclockwise movement of the Gulf waters. On the eastern fringe the young lobsters traveled as much as a hundred miles to the peninsula shore, and some settled and survived among the doomed oysters. Many, however, were victims of late timing and current changes, and these youngsters fell into the mid-Gulf trench and died immediately.

Fewer than ten lobsters out of every hundred would survive the free-swimming time. They would suffer massive mortality as they awaited that invulnerable time when, equipped with horny carapaces, heavy claws, and cunning, few water hunters would dare to touch them. Now as helpless victims in the plankton, they were merely a resource of the sea, placed there to be eaten. At dusk they descended from the surface but were taken by herring when they came up to feed. The young lobsters who fell to the bottom dropped into the waiting territorial demands of crabs and small fishes and, dishonorably, resident adult lobsters. These youngsters were decimated before they were allowed to occupy one inch of the sea bottom.

Those who survived molting at the perilous bottom and lived to acquire hard shells and claws would have to face cod and skates and dogfish. Only after five years of growth and molt would they acquire the arrogance that grows everywhere behind massive armor.

V

It was time for the mackerel. Cool winds, bright sun, sudden mists—early summer kissed the Gulf. After five days of slow drifting in the southern Gulf the mackerel eggs hatched. The youngsters, vulnerable as individuals, schooled quickly and created a dense mass of fish two miles long. In sixty days all of them would be a uniform two inches long. Mackerel hatched later would stick to their own brotherhood, held forever by that coincidence of birth time, and they would winter and hunt and mature and eventually spawn in these segregated schools.

In this early period, however, they suffered grievous mortality. Gulls based in shoreline and island colonies harried them during all daylight hours. The murres and prowling puffins, fortunately not so thick in the southern Gulf, pursued them. The giant cod's memory was infallible, and up he came from the bottom with many smaller cod, and they all dashed among the juvenile mackerel, filling their stomachs again and again. Squid joined them, but the mackerel were not routed. They handled these hunters by sacrifice and comradeship. They would stick together through this summer and fall and would migrate with the other mackerel, each age group separate, to find offshore sanctuaries outside the Gulf during the winter months. And when they returned it would be their turn to destroy.

The burgeoning populations of young fish were dissident voices in the Gulf. Whenever they prowled in their masses they caused friction and alarm, savage hunting and change. Young herring pressed against the Gulf in such numbers that they became the reason for migrations and routs, and they left behind them new commonwealths of creatures born out of their flesh and their success.

VI

Most of the Gulf's children were born as eggs, but a few were born alive: mice in forest burrows and aerial homes; squirrels in tree-top nests; foxes in riverbank dens; raccoons in hollow trees; skunks in groundhog burrows; wolves in caves, watchful in the territory of the cave-loving cougar. The live births of the Gulf demonstrated how to survive those anxious first days when the inexperienced children must learn about their enemies.

The caribou of the big island, collected in the upland breeding grounds, all calved in one intense period. As they bore their young, wolves appeared like gray ghosts in the early-morning light and struck into the herds at many points, always selecting peripheral calves, the least well protected, the sacrificial calves, themselves born of peripheral parents.

The caribou moved and the wolves remained attendant, forcing the caribou into larger and larger coalitions. This did not deter the wolves. Thirty days hence they would find it easy to strike into very large herds, stampede them, and so cut down the larger calves. In this way the stragglers, the panickers, the unwise, and the weak were sorted out of the herd and eaten.

The lynx, with his own kittens suckling in a den at

the foot of mountain cliffs, had no concern for them. He had separated entirely from his mate during this rearing time and hunted alone. He watched the wolves at dusk as they glided along forest trails and heard the crash and snort of caribou beset. He watched partridge chicks pecking at the grassy fringes of a stream, independent from the moment they left the egg. Seeing him, they melted instantly into the grass and were gone. The hares, the elusives, were now gray-brown, and still elusive. The lynx pushed into a thicket, nostrils twitching, movements silent. The thump of a hare's foot, a scattering of invisible animals. Eyes intent, he moved toward a nestful of young hares crouched in a hollow. A sniff. The hares scattered like the partridges, and the lynx's paws smashed down three times, striking bare earth. Silence. The hares were gone.

The Gulf observed its children impartially as they struggled for a place in the sea or on land. A female shark entered the Gulf through the southern strait and was almost inside her greatest summer hunting grounds when she was struck sidelong by a playful killer whale. She reeled away, spouting blood, to die. Involuntarily, her children were born, a score of sharklings who disappeared in a few moments into the green depths. A blue whale paused in the northern strait and bore her single youngster, who suckled twenty gallons of milk from its mother as the two of them cruised north toward the arctic. The pilot whales, gorged for the moment on squid, collected in herds off the eastern shore of the big island and bore their youngsters, who would all be free within ten days, when they joined their parents in communal hunting. The coastal seals whelped on beaches everywhere, but particularly along the western shore of the Gulf where the salmon were still collecting in the shallows in readiness for their river-spawning runs.

Live birth rather than egg birth was not restricted to the higher animals of the Gulf. In two thousand feet of water, in the middle of the Gulf, the female redfish were now ready to give birth. Each female had up to forty thousand eggs inside her body nearly ready to hatch. The redfish, although resident in the black depths, knew something about the survival of eggs at such a depth and through the years had held the eggs longer and longer inside their bodies. Now they hatched, still not born but swelling inside their mother's bodies until birth could not be delayed. Out they poured, tiny replicas of their parents, and immediately headed for the surface half a mile distant. They left the relative warmth of the deeps, moved into a cold arctic layer which was still lurking in memory of winter, escaped from it before they froze to death, crossed a barrier of almost salt-free water thrust there by western rivers, and finally entered the surface waters, where they joined the plankton. They would hunt among the plankton until they were an inch long, whereupon, responding to ancient orders, they would return to the depths whence they had come.

143

VII

The white eagle turned downwind and swept west along the northern shore. Offshore islands, dull shoreline jewels, roared and cackled with seabird hostility. An island, white as frost and already spuming up thousands of gannets who rose to attack him, hurried the eagle away. He glided faster than any gannet could hope to fly, and saw that the island was packed with gawky gannet children, as helpless as any youngsters in the Gulf. But they were forever beyond his reach because of their guardian parents. Another island sped underneath, specked with watchful puffins who ignored him, having no need to attack an enemy who could not reach their children safe underground. The gulls of the islands, spaced regularly along the shore, reacted to him with outrage, fury, and hate, and he skirted them, safely distant from furious eyes and flailing wings, while below, sharp in his eyes, young gulls walked the island as unconcerned as though he were harmless. Eider ducks fled one island, quietly and anonymously, and so deft was their departure that the eagle would never know they had left behind many nests full of ducklings, scantily hidden under eider down. He saw ducklings strung out across the shoreline Gulf like beads attached to their mothers, and despite his height, they saw and feared him, and disappeared, leaving a hundred identical dimples of water.

The Gulf smiled on the seabirds and welcomed their myriad children, and the eagle became a point of furious expectation in the western sky.

Chapter NINE

I

Hunters moved into the Gulf and the slaughter began. Thresher sharks flailed great waving tails like whips and herded herring into tight groups. They rounded up the mackerel and squid, whipped them into panicky congregations, then cut them to pieces. White sharks swiftly crossed the Gulf and began a summer-long search for shoreline seals. As the seals were thinned the sharks filtered down the western shore to find the sturgeon waiting to enter their rivers, and scattered them. They met tuna hurrying up the shore, and destroyed them.

Blue sharks, less deadly but more catholic in their

tastes, made a shambles of herring herds and mackerel schools at the surface, then dived, and the haddock and pollack and cod fled for their lives. Spiny dogfish crowded the estuaries and chased salmon. They prowled plateau waters and rounded up the cod. They chased pollack into such panic that the fish threw themselves at the shore and landed on beaches. The spiny dogfish ate everything: cod and mackerel, herring and capelin, whelk and jellyfish, shrimp and crab, and turned the Gulf hunt into a homicidal vendetta. The giant cod, remembering these summer murderers, dropped away to the deepest trench he knew and grazed on small starfish.

The hunters advanced from the south; they came up out of the depths; they rained down from the skies; they ran on silent forest feet. A wolf's night cry on the big island, a long rising call that told the caribou they must die, held its tone against a melancholy moon and sank to a whisper as the caribou cringed. The big cats of the southern shore padded pine needles in darkness and killed up to five hundred deer a night. The peregrine falcons spread themselves thinly along every shore, keeping careful distance between one another. They raided small seabird colonies, cut down landbirds flying to favorite islands, and obliterated small family groups of guillemots and razorbills. They persuaded the creatures of the shore to accept a balance they had not made themselves. In the forest a sparrowhawk passed at the robin's ear with such speed he felt the wind and heard the whistle of the projectile but saw nothing. The sparrowhawk flung into a thicket

147

and curved through it, a wren in his talon. In a moment he would take one of the robin's three surviving nestlings, now cautiously free from the nest.

The hunters were everywhere at once: crows on beaches awaiting exhausted landbirds during migrations; great horned owls warning restless crows how dangerous were these summer nights; cod rampaging among the capelin; haddock gorging on eggs and flatfish grazing on oceanic bottoms. A small group of walrus pushed into the Gulf through the northern strait, the last of a great herd which had once exploited and almost wiped out a central Gulf shellfish nation. Their ton-weight bodies cruised the bottom and they bit off the morsel-sized necks of clams. They crushed scallop shells, sucked out the meat, and spat out the shells, but it was clams that drew them most. Once, in the prime of their history, they had taken half a million tons of shellfish flesh in a year, the reason for their poverty now.

The hunt diversified, and touched every life in the Gulf amid bright suns and whispering water and cool-warm breezes, and skies blue enough to match a jay's wing. Small whales—minkes—came inshore in pursuit of the capelin, savaged them mercilessly when they reeled offshore after spawning, and scattered them wide in the sea. The pilot whales, following the squid, broke away for a moment and added to the capelin rout. The lynx looked for his share of hares, one every second night, and the lobster upended the familiar shellfish and chipped away until he could smash the well-broken shell flat with

148

his crunching claw.

The hunt was the Gulf's blood, pumping red and fierce through the vessels of its body.

II

At noon the southern strait thrust up sharp-edged blades. The fins of swordfish cruised deliberately into the Gulf in a school spread across a two-mile front. The swordfish were not interested in individual fish, and in the three months they chose to spend in the Gulf they would brush them aside as they sped forward. They sought schools. They hunted for herring swarms in their manifold Gulf migrations. They hunted capelin inshore. They found silver hake and argentines and lancetfish. At night they attacked squid massing at the surface to feed. Occasionally the redfish came cautiously out of their deep strongholds in the center of the Gulf, and the swordfish knew this and met them at the surface.

The swordfish spread out into the Gulf and formed into loose-knit groups that found disciplined satisfaction in united hunting. Their attacks were a distillation of the hunt: brutal, deadly, effective. They hit with a sudden rush of slender, powerful bodies, and their furious flailing at the surface seemed without purpose until the water was red with death. Then their leisurely feeding filled air and sea with attendant scavengers. Gulls hastened from shore and island to feed and squabble at the surface. Cod rose from the bottom to find the source of this rain of debris. At the bottom, the lobster fed on refugee pieces.

Each swordfish attack was orderly, set in motion by a leader who swam ahead of his comrades, his eyes cocked upward for fish silhouetted against the surface. On sighting herring, he heaved to the surface and hurled himself six feet into the air. A thousand pounds of glistening flight held for a moment, then twisted in a rain of water drops and foam. He whiplashed his body sharply in midair so that it landed flat. The concussion of his fall stunned many fish and panicked all the others. But the flailing and the churning and the blood and the other swordfish hastening to the kill were secondary moments to the drama of the original attack.

III

The giant cod skulked in his trench and let the hunt sweep harmlessly above him. His hunger, as usual, drove him back and forth across a shellfish colony, and his victims, killed so systematically, became hard to find, and so increased his hunger.

The dictate of the cod hunt was not a single order. It was a combination of thousands of forces and conditions, and the cod reacted differently to every part of the Gulf. No one codfish nation hunted the same way as any other, since each nation was subject to different influences of currents, the times of spawning, and the supply of various sources of food. Now, with the summer begun, cod were pouring into the Gulf through the southern strait from their winter residence along submarine slopes south of the big island. Other cod rode the currents into the Gulf through the northern strait, traveling light and shallow and making three to four hundred miles in six days.

Cod were adaptable, omnivorous, aggressive. Their look-alike colleagues, the haddock, were much more conservative and predictable, and so the cod outnumbered them many times. The cod stomach testified to his adaptability and showed why the different nations of cod occupied so much of the Gulf in such overwhelming numbers. The cod of the northern strait, the coldest and most turbulent water in the Gulf, were bottom prowlers nearly all year, often ranging down to stygian depths in pursuit of spider crabs. They ate amphipods and pteropods, sparse hunting sometimes, but no other fish competed there.

Deeper into the Gulf, along the western coast of the big island, the hunting was easier. The cod flourished there, at first on launce and then on capelin, most of the summer. The cod of the southern Gulf relished lobsters and swallowed them whole, tail first so that the claws were nipped shut in the cod's throat as they went down. South of the big island, in the deep waters between the island and an offshore plateau, scallop beds attracted the cod in

151

millions, the giant cod among them. The scallops were swallowed whole and their shells coughed out in careless heaps.

The cod hunted in age groups, and their habits changed as they grew older, more experienced—and hungrier because of their swelling bulk. As a youngster the giant cod had collected with millions of his own age on the central Gulf plateau, and, as befit his inexperience, he was conservative. He and his comrades never moved more than two hundred miles in any direction from their places of birth along the southern fringes of the plateau. As small fish they had been able to find sustenance everywhere across the plateau, feeding on the teeming crustaceans.

But the hunt became more complex as the cod grew. At three years of age he had to range wider and seek new foods. Crustaceans would not fill his belly. He ranged hundreds of miles in summer in search of larger prey, and more of it. As a six-year-old, beset by hunger, he had fled the plateau territory and made a desperate, surface-water dash east through the southern strait and out of the Gulf. There, far offshore, he had nearly starved to death before he was caught in a western current which took him inshore again into collision with herring. Gradually he moved back into the Gulf that summer, but lost the herring in the fall. He moved again, impelled by his immense hunger, and struck north, up the western shores of the big island. Fortuitously, he found winter nations of launce, and he survived.

The search for food dominated everything. It sent

him through the northern strait into the influence of the arctic, where he ate young cod drifting south. He came down the eastern coast of the big island and ate lobster and shrimp and capelin and launce and herring and sculpin. He found the young cod along the island's shores, as vulnerable as he had been years before, and he hunted them. He found the great scallop beds south of the island, and so he survived, mobile and aggressive, and followed his appetite in eternal search for enough.

IV

The hunter intertwined the limbs of its creatures and made them brothers, even though they killed each other to survive. The Gulf was indulgent; the sun was warm and the winds gentle. The tides withdrew and exposed rippled sandbanks. White cliffs threw down reflections and the seabirds laughed at what they found there. An airborne shellfish turned slowly against the sun in a seabird's bill and cracked open on a rock.

The shellfish of the Gulf, like the plankton and herring and capelin, were a crude resource. The clam that fed the walrus had brothers who fed wolffish and flounder and crabs and whelks and seagulls and a host of others. The sands of the western and southern shores, the narrow beaches around the big island, and the mud estuaries were shellfish headquarters where a different drama of the hunt was enacted. This was no bloody raw thrust of violence, but sly and slow.

On the beaches the sand jumped with surf clams, who pumped blood in and out of feet that protruded like tongues from between their shells. With the wind brisk and jolly and the overcast scudding against the moon, the clams flipped along in a series of angry jerks. But these walking, shelled creatures were not protected. Under the sand, boring relentlessly forward, predatory whelks pushed themselves like mindless machines which fueled on clams.

The sands of the Gulf were no less dangerous than the sea where hunters could strike from any direction, but in the sand hunting went on in absurd slow motion. Smooth whelks bored in endless pursuit of soft-shell clams, their appetites nicely balanced against the hunting of gulls for both the whelks and the clams, and both were often taken together, the one trying to eat the other.

At night the whelks stole time from the gulls by hunting the surface of the sand at low tide. If they found a clam early in the night they bored a hole through his shell, inserted a proboscis, and cleaned out the living flesh. But if they made the catch late at night they understood there was no time to bore and eat before the appearance of the dreaded gulls. So they raised a bump on the back of their walking feet, placed the tightly shut clam there, and then dug to safety as the day-hunting gulls began their work. The whelks ranged wide. They did not merely hunt at low tide, but were active at high tide among the massed armies of blue mussels clinging to littoral rocks. They drilled their single, deadly holes, ate, and passed on.

In the everlasting shellfish hunt, no clam was safe. Clam hunters never forgot the taste of that flesh, and they had refined and sharpened their techniques. The flounder of the southern Gulf shallows, moving inshore in spring to feed, saw the breathing necks of buried clams and neatly nipped them off. Eels, waiting in estuaries to ascend rivers, searched out the clams, grabbed their necks, and fought a fierce fight until the neck was wrenched out of the clam body by its roots. The clams might recover from a flounder attack, mending the damage with scar tissue and managing to continue breathing, but the eel attack was fatal. The clams tried desperately not to die. They moved up in the sand and half revealed their shells. They tried to breathe through the gaping holes in their bodies, but they could not get enough water filtered through their nets to keep them fat. They drew on body fat; their shells disintegrated and became thin and transparent. So, still breathing hard, they died of starvation.

This year green crabs were ascendant at the southern shore, recent migrants from the south, and they carried the hunt to the clams with great efficiency. They sensed the position of the buried clam and dug down to it, working steadily at the sand face thus exposed: down, down, down. The digging crab was rarely alone. Behind and above him two sand shrimps, swimming in the debris of the digging, waited for a chance to feed on the small chunks of flesh the crab might miss after he had reached

155

the clam, chipped away a corner of the shell, and shredded the body before eating it.

The clams were victims of their own succulence, but were any shellfish less vulnerable? Brainless starfish moved with muscles bulging and body fluids pumping out their arms; with suction cups ready to grip and pull and strangle and smother; with each foot connected by nerve networks to the others so that each knew what the others were doing. They came up out of sheltering sea valleys and headed for the oyster beds. They came in waves, their populations rising and falling with enigmatic rapidity. Sometimes they were so abundant in the southern shallows that shellfish there were annihilated, with mussels the most vulnerable.

The starfish spread out among the oysters. A starfish settled like a shroud over each oyster and fastened hundreds of suckers to the shell. All around him bodies bowed, bent, pulled and pulled. The starfish had many muscles, the oyster had only one. The oyster muscle tired first. Shells gaped, and starfish stomachs came out of their bodies and entered the oyster shells. They consumed the oysters alive.

The standfasts in the Gulf faced their enemies stoically. They were accustomed to the hunter arriving and boring, or pulling, or shoving, or scrunching. Boring sponges, residents of the Gulf's southern shallows where oysters, barnacles, and scallops thrived, attacked nearly all shellfish and were only repelled by the mussels, whose horny outer shells gave them a defense.

The oysters suffered most. The hunt of the sponges

was so far advanced among some oysters that millions of cripples clung loosely to life after the sponges had drilled complexes of tunnels and galleries throughout the shells and left only scattered pillars to hold the two thin pieces of outer and inner shell apart.

The oysters fought the invaders this summer by patching the sponge holes on the inner surface with temporary filler. This might give the oyster time to manufacture limy shell, which would plug the holes permanently. Some of the older oysters were weakening after years of boring attacks. The sponges had eaten them hollow and were now boring into the shell where the hinge ligament and muscle were fastened at the center. Healthy oysters used the muscle to pull the shell closed and compress the rubbery ligament. This ligament, resilient, tough, and compressed, sprung the shell open whenever the muscle was relaxed. When the boring sponges damaged the muscle they made it impossible for the shell to close. When they damaged the ligament the oyster could not open the shell and so choked to death. The oysters died with the Gulf flowering above them, died with their jaws locked in some awful clamp which paralyzed them but left the sponges to continue their work undisturbed. The muscle-struck oysters died more quickly. They gaped and yielded to fish, and their shells went spinning away across the sea bottom. The lobster feasted and the sponges tunneled on, oblivious.

V

The first sound of a wolffish bringing his powerful jaws down on a scallop shell sent the nearby scallops into flight and demonstrated that shellfish need not remain helpless victims. The squid, who were also shellfish, took this notion two steps further: it was not only possible to escape the hunters, it was also possible to *become* hunters, to exceed the rapacity and success of the creatures who had plagued them. By any measurement they were superb instruments of the hunt: tubular, streamlined, with a tri-angular-shaped vane for controlling depth and direction at one end of their bodies. A thick mass of arms sprouted from the other end, and they jet-propelled themselves hydraulically at such speed that a rushing attack of squid was almost too fast for any eye in the sea to follow.

Such an extraordinary escape from the fortress shell had not been accomplished without penalty, however. The squid attacked best backward. They drove their tri-vaned tails into schools of herring, flashing past their victims' head at such speed that the herring had no time to jerk away before the squid mouth was turned at their heads and a piece of herring body was bitten clean from the shoulder.

The squid were the most mysterious hunters, their

origins obscure. The other hunters were simply traced to some other sea or hemisphere or gulf, but the squid came instead from unknowable and distant deep water. Probably they wintered far south of the big island, in mid-ocean abysses. They had appeared in late spring south of the island, their advance rippling the surface over square miles of water, each creature four inches long and feeding exclusively on the blooming euphausids. The squid collected, dispersed, moved forward and backward, and vacuumed the surface like mackerel. After their passage few organisms remained alive on the surface.

The vigor of their hunting was so great that they soon outgrew that place and were impelled into the Gulf in ancient pursuit of the next source of food. The pilot whales were their constant companions, though not their friends, and took a thousand tons of them each day. But this was only a pinprick in their vast corporation.

The euphausids fell astern and the squid passed through the strait and fell among the capelin who had just finished spawning inshore. They swept through the capelin, chopping and churning the surface, and moved on, now at the surface and moving very fast. They approached the big island's shores, surrounded small islands lying offshore from it, and fell among herring. In minutes, square miles of sea were filled with shredded herring flesh. This was the squids' first sight of land, and it took them by surprise. Thousands were stranded on beaches during the first two nights of their arrival. The remainder, hovering offshore, observed the danger of the land and learned to avoid it, and the strandings stopped.

From midsummer onward the squid would prowl the coasts of the island. They would alter all life wherever their massive host touched. They would grow at high speed, attacking larger and larger prey, small cod wrenched to pieces, redfish sundered and torn, haddock pursued and butchered, in an inshore hunt that would continue until the fall.

VI

The hunt went on throughout the Gulf. The lynx sent a hare fleeing away into the dusk and stopped and keened at her thumping departure. Then he sat and purred and licked his paws and scratched himself, and waited. His hunger was not demanding yet. In a minute he turned and flattened, and crouch-ran forward. The hare, running hard from her oldest enemy, never felt the skull-breaking blow, never would understand that her enemy knew she ran in circles and had waited for her return to the place where she had been flushed.

The plankton blossomed and divided and copulated, and the herring and capelin thrived on its growth. Cod came charging to the surface in pursuit of small fish and fell among the squid, and recovered strength by eating them.

160

The mackerel, all-ingesting cleaners of the surface, took everything with them: herring and shrimp and copepods. The largest commonwealth of mackerel, two-year-olds swinging across the southern shallows, collided with a hatching of eggs of the six-year-old mackerel. The hatching mackerel were destroyed. The two-year-olds passed on, replete, soon to be hunting other plankton, crab larvae, amphipods, launce, and whatever else they might meet at the surface.

Mackerel and herring, capelin and squid, lobster and clam, whale and krill, codfish and dogfish, haddock and plaice, diatom and ctenophore, crab and whelk, worm and sponge, walrus and seal, shark and seabird—the rhythms of the hunt echoed and re-echoed through the Gulf. The slaughter went on exuberantly, and the Gulf thrived, laughing and excited, as it had never thrived before.

Chapter TEN

I

The summer of the Gulf grew ripe and expanded north to include every living creature. It buoyed up the eagle on columns of uprushing air, burnished the northern strait with a sun possessing temporary tropical heat, and broke the coldest shadows into acceptance of the season. High summer paused; every creature was emplaced. Forest creepers had stuck nests to strips of spruce bark and orioles' sacks hung loose and noisy with young birds from the highest branches. Young robins drank from glistening stones in warming rivers and ignorant, gawky gulls looked dubiously down from cliff tops. The harp seals reached their arctic country, joined narwhals and walrus in sportive passage among silent edifices of ice, still life in glassy seas. The southern roadway of the migrants of the Gulf was empty and silent. The last of the mackerel millions had entered the Gulf, and the codfish were done with their seasonal reaching for new territories. The caribou plodded across the high country of the big island and browsed on spruce tips.

The forests breathed, processing water and gases, their function uniform over a hundred thousand square miles of land that surrounded the Gulf and was under its influence. The Gulf itself, another hundred thousand square miles of water-giving energy without which the forests could not survive, lay placid. Instead of roaring and weeping in wind and rain, the forests whispered to the soul sounds of seven billion trees. Hemlocks and spruces, firs and pines, maples and beeches, oaks and tamaracks—seven billion factories of sap and chlorophyll, refuges for birds, insects and mammals. Trees gregarious but committing genocide and regicide and infanticide. Beneath their sheltering arms another seven billion juvenile trees pushed, strained, groaned upward against the insupportable burden of their parents. These youngsters of the forest, and especially the youthful trees in the old forests of the western shore, were doubly urgent, doubly ambitious for the kind of revolution they knew must lie just ahead.

The forests were fat with summer, yet never had they worked harder to withdraw water from the earth and spray the Gulf with a perpetual light rain. Under the invisible rain huddled thirty billion shrubs, packed among the trees and strung along the riverbanks and in places where trees had fallen: rhododendrons and hobblebushes, gooseberries and scinberries and the ambitious dogwood. The shrubs were themselves protectors and colleagues of three thousand billion plants, creeping herbaceous lives that clung close enough to the Gulf earth to be utterly anonymous, like the sorrel and the corn lilies, or slightly bolder foamflowers and asters, cranberries, blueberries, and bayberries. The ubiquitous ferns reached almost every place, at the edge of every stream and brook.

The Gulf breathed through these lives and the sun became tropically hot. It burned into the trees with an imperious hard light that made the forests gasp, and each tree, host to thousands of insects, suffered these tiny creatures creeping and crawling and leaping and burrowing and sucking and chiseling in a concerted effort to eat, suck out all juice, defoliate, cram in eggs and larvae and pupae. The trees had to protect these flying armies and sustain them in every way, even as they were attacked.

The most destructive of them, the aphids, swarmed in the heat in all their multitudinous forms, winged and wingless, and attacked everywhere, destroying twigs and foliage, and produced a dozen generations piled rapidly on top of one another. Green, bloated, creeping, six-legged, they were the spirit of all infestations. The white eagle, hovering very high, saw the tops of forests which had died under the onslaught of their sucking.

164

Sawflies and horntails ranged through many forests, their long yellow-ringed bodies distinctive in the summer sun, double wings invisible as they searched for places to bury their eggs in dead and living wood, eggs which mostly hatched out leaf-eating larvae that defoliated tamaracks and larches and which, in their only concession to the forests, ate the old foliage of balsam firs and spruces and jackpines as well.

The trees crawled with insects. Great green luna moths lay silent at the robin's ear this night while the polyphemus moths, larger than warblers, crossed dark clearings and their children spread among the hickories and maples and birches of the western shore. The moths twisted silently, sphinxes and prometheas, imperials and satins, while all around them their caterpillars ate away at almost every tree and shrub. By day the moth dance was taken over by the empty-headed butterflies in all their exuberant colors: copper, purple, blue, russet, sulphur, black, yellow, red. And *their* caterpillars ate the forests with the juvenile moth hordes.

The forests were hosts, refuges, arenas for the hunter and the hunted. They gave shelter to birds who pursued this insect horde and who were, indeed, the only defense the trees had against destruction. Through their leafy arms flew the birds—hurtling flickers and noisy nuthatches, vireos and kinglets, warblers and juncoes, sparrows and thrushes, ovenbirds and wrens—in search of spiders and beetles, worms and caterpillars, aphids and flies.

The robin paused, held uncertain by all he saw, the

165

forest jigging and jogging with things to eat. He hesitated, selected a caterpillar, and plucked it from a leaf, hovering for a second like a hummingbird, then dropped back to his perch. The summer was good, the Gulf was good. He was alive in an earthstream of life.

II

The Gulf of summer piled creatures into a pyramid of numbers. A few creatures sat on top: the white eagle, killer whales, the torpedoing wolves ringing one caribou. Their weight helped keep the creatures underneath well crushed, submissive in body if restless in spirit. The millions of forest birds around the Gulf made sacrifices to mere thousands of hawks and owls, a constant monthly attrition of a million of the bird population.

Thousands of caribou plodded among the wolves, who were steady in the hundreds, giving no hint of why they remained constant in number. The lynx shared the Gulf with thousands of other lynx, feeding on the millions of hares. Hundreds of thousands of foxes lived in uneasy balance with billions of mice, who, burdened like the trees, helped to support the millions of raccoons and skunks and other creatures as well as the thousands of black bears.

In the Gulf itself, at this high point of summer, the

166

pyramid of numbers encompassed at least a billion cod-fish swarming, millions of haddock and flatfish, too many herring to count, forty miles of blue-eyed scallops breathing deeply of the arctic, hundreds of millions of oysters wary among a million starfish who each ate one oyster every seven days. Tens of thousands of swordfish swam with hundreds of blue whales. A few thousand pilot whales ate a thousand tons of squid each day—but there were billions of squid.

The pyramid of numbers towered over the Gulf, dwarfing the wars and peaces, the couplings and spawnings. Cougars, one pair to each ridge of forest, took out several hundred white-tailed deer each day. The songbirds of all the Gulf built millions of nests and laid more than a billion eggs, but they raised less than half a billion nestlings, and many of these were short-lived. The seabirds laid millions of eggs, but managed to raise little more than half that number as nestlings. Of these youngsters half again would die within the year.

The Gulf gathered its creatures in protective arms, made for them a most perfect place, and then executed them.

III

The lynx peered out of the den entrance, out into a forest whispering with life: birds crying, ravens circling, and, in the distance, the slap of salmon jumping. Perfect summer touched every life but, in puzzling contradiction, missed the lynx. Amber eyes hurt, he looked into the bright day and swallowed his hunger. Sixteen nights of hunting: no hares. Empty moonlight mocked him: no furtive thump of a distant hare foot. He could not live without hares, and he had almost exhausted the possibilities of paltry mouse hunting and of birds' nests clawed from trees. But the hares were not there; he could not range far enough at night now to find them, and his hunger weakened him. The hares were missing in his world of night. He dreamed of hares, fantasmic throngs of them leaping across moonlit clearings, and he awoke shaking. But the true hares had gone.

His family starved in their den, his mate's sides pressed thin against her ribs, the kits mewing rage at the slender flow of milk. All lynxes knew this should be the greatest time of hares—stupid, incautious hares; exuberant, prolific hares leaping from their mothers' wombs and into the jaws of the lynx, flooding lynx country with their bodies. Only days ago the hares had jumped from every clump of grass, but those days were yesterday.

Three years before, the hares of the Gulf had begun one of their customary great population growths, and their added millions had made lynxes a little mad all around the Gulf. Weak lynxes survived. Old lynxes not only survived but bred beyond their allotted span. In three years the lynxes had doubled their numbers, and the hunting had never been so easy.

The Gulf bestowed, but it would not tolerate such imbalance within its corporation. The hares had to adjust their numbers to conform to the order of the Gulf, and this silent imperative was executed first in the territory of the hungry lynx. The hares there crashed, plummeting from their population peak down through a catastrophic numbers game which swept them away like flies in a hurricane. The lynx, no carrion-lover, tentatively lifted parchment-dry pelts and dimly sensed his prey escaping him, leaping just beyond reach of his big-booted claws. He ranged wider, circled bears scrunching old hare bones, saw bloated hare bodies eddying down rivers. He fought other lynx in spitting, yowling recognition of mutual hunger and, well beyond his care, two of his kittens died as the second step in the restoration of the correct place of lynx and hare at the Gulf.

From this kind of hunger a special desperation grew. A family group of caribou drank at the river, and the lynx watched them. Three calves stamped their feet and shook their heads as big, blood-sucking flies clustered at their hocks and noses, and the lynx watched them. That night,

169

when the caribou paused in a tight family group at the top of a ridge, they smelled lynx and moved restlessly. They smelled lynx from the south and from the west, and the bull caribou leading the group snorted and struck his feet in the ground in warning.

Unlike the wolf, the lynx attack came in a silent, flying form which clamped itself onto the face of a caribou calf who had turned a few steps away from the family group. He went to his knees with needle claws in his eyeballs. Another attacker struck his rear legs just above the knees, and teeth ripped his tendons. Hamstrung, he fell, and the bull caribou whirled toward him, feet upraised. But there was neither sight nor sound of the attackers. The forest was silent except for a distant owl call. One of the cows heard and smelled the soft swish of blood, and lost herd obedience. She bolted down the slope, two calves following her. The bull whirled again, indecisive for the moment. Then he went after them. The rest crashed along behind.

The crippled calf tried to drag himself away, but hamstrung and blinded, he could do little except kick. He heard nothing, but in a moment invisible teeth found his throat.

IV

Ostensibly, the summer was a time of pause when the rigors of winter and the impatience of spring were softened in a flood of food. Abundance, however, was a theoretical benefit. Sudden abundance in any part of the Gulf presaged sudden changes, disorders, revolutions, catastrophes in almost exactly the same way as did shortage.

The plankton of a western bay rested in the palm of summer but found its warmth uncomfortable. The dominant plankton—copepods which were feeding the bay's herring—dropped fifty feet and found a cooler layer of water. But this layer was moving contrary to the circling surface, impelled by a combination of river outflow and the rotation of the earth. In ten days of growing warmth the copepods were carried out of the bay and sent slowly spinning down the western shore of the Gulf.

Willy-nilly, the herring must follow. They streamed out of the bay, and seabirds, accustomed to their regular surfacings, hovered uncertainly over the empty waters. In three days all of this herring nation was gone out of the bay and was well strung out along the shore. They fattened rapidly on the copepod host, itself increasing rapidly. Fifty miles south the copepods ran into an upswelling cold current, which put them to sleep. They fell, disappearing

171

into bottom ooze. The herring, having been brought so far, backed up against the upswelling cold and formed a dense mass of fish nearly a score of miles long. The leaders hesitated, then drove for the surface, but found it empty, and so dived again. But the copepods had gone completely.

After four days of searching, feeding on their own body fat, the herring accidentally fell among a southward-moving population of euphausids, the tiny shrimplike krill so well liked by whales and seabirds. They were attended by the petrel and her kind, who were converting the krill into the rich oil with which they fed their island nestlings. The euphausids gave the herring nation movement and purpose, and the herring ate so well that they left a track in the sea, a glittering, multicolored oil slick of excrement laden with the life juices of the creatures they were eating. In this way the herring swung down toward the southern shallows of the Gulf and disappeared from their bay.

This summer would not see the end of their journey. Once set in motion, once removed from the rigid regimes of their bay, they were liberated but also transformed into travelers who *must* continue their journey. They would drift with the euphausids; they would endure attacks by whales who had meetings arranged with the euphausids thirty days hence; they would winter uneasily in the southern shallows and suffer the seals and the cod and the seabirds. They would join the drifting oyster larvae in the spring of the following year, but because of a slightly different depth of drift they would push out into the middle of the southern strait instead of spilling out of the Gulf.

172

This would turn them in a grand northwestern curve, and they would be cut to pieces by mackerel entering the Gulf. They would spend the summer among surfacing shrimp, drifting larval cod, and haddock. With the onset of fall and the disappearance of surface life, they would sink toward a wintering place at the bottom but would find nothing but endless black depths. Through the winter the great herring nation would melt away, like submarine snow, dead from the attrition of their freedom.

Behind them, in the bay, the traditional rhythms would long since have been re-established. New herring populations would turn in the bay as though the lost generation had never lived.

V

With the herring well set on their fatal two-year journey and the hungry lynx lifting his bloodstained whiskers from a caribou carcass, benign summer showed its other face at the Gulf. Only the Gulf itself seemed secure, yet fifteen thousand years of tyrannical ice made suspect all notions of security, even for the Gulf.

The lobster moved from his sheltering rock, fat behind his hard green sheath, his sperm deposited and he too big to be bitten by seals: big enough to contest any cod.

His comrades thrived. Greenish-blue bodies half hid

under stones; reddish-brown carapaces glistened in the half light of the shallows, huge claws at menacing repose, swimmerets trembling and tails poised to whisk away in flight.

The lobster moved into clear ground and raised his claws. A cod drifting nearby, four times his size, backed away. His claws, those archaic extensions of his castle walls, were his only connection with subtlety. His right claw was a crusher, massive and developed to break up shellfish, shred large fish, or crush crabs. He was right-clawed. His left claw, his quick claw, was smaller and much lighter. It flicked now, and a small fish disappeared from midwater.

The ingenuity of his claws was shared in other forms by his comrades. Some were left-clawed, with the quick claw on the right, while others had two quick claws. A few, very odd this, had two crushing claws. The claws of the lobsters were their only admission that times might change, that the future might favor the quick claws, or the crushers, or the left claws.

The lobster felt the unbearable pressure of his big body pushing against his shell. It did not matter how much the Gulf assured him that it was summer, the good time; this was the worst moment of his life, and he must hasten to it. He must drop the walls, leave his security, and build a new home. The fortress shell did not grow, but the lobster did, very much like the cod, a victim of his life-long appetite which placed no limit on his size.

On tiptoe he glided over rocks into a shallow gully

174

littered with weeds and used his claws to throw the weeds up and burrow under them as if he were remembering another age when his naked crisis could be passed hidden from view.

The weeds heaved, and his body appeared. He stood very tall, his claws held out, swimmerets trembling. His shell had dulled and a reddish tint had developed at each of his many joints. All along the underside of his tail and the middle of his back his shell had gone soft. In one slow, graceful movement he folded his legs and rolled on his side. A pale membrane joining his hard back and segmented tail split, and the split widened.

The giant cod reached the southern Gulf shallows, bound on a journey of five hundred miles and vastly irritated at his hunger, his body burning up its own flesh. He had an old memory of lobster molting, an imperfect one, but his time clock was accurate. He missed the main body of molting lobsters fringing the coast, but he reached a gully and saw a lobster there, his shell split wide and his body jackknifing, heaving and straining into view.

The lobster's body was wrinkled and old-looking, a travesty of that bold fellow who had emerged from the weeds a moment ago. He must now absorb water rapidly to fatten up the wrinkled, useless claws and then find refuge to await the hardening of new fortress walls.

He had just disengaged his tail from the slit of the old shell when the giant cod hit him. It was a fair bite, an explosion of tissue flaming away from it, and the lobster's tail kicked away among the rocks and his head somer-

175

saulted in the other direction. The giant cod took his time, perhaps considering whether to bother with the two morsels remaining. After a second he turned and ate the tail piece, then snuffled up the head section and disappeared in search of another molter.

The discarded shell—was it still *him?*—lay inert, the gap in its back closed, its sightless eyestalks looking at nothing. The shell was an end of summer, in one of its forms, and it was repeated elsewhere in the Gulf. Empty shells rolled in the tides and currents, empty reminders of these empty lives.

Chapter ELEVEN

I

The Gulf was in flight from long ice winters and now, in secure warmth, some of its functions were revealed as disorders which it could neither arbitrate nor control. Hot air gathered in conspiratorial hollows and plotted the rape of cold-loving creatures of the Gulf. Warm water flowed in Gulf veins and killed innocents with its smothering kindness. The Gulf remained aloof while these catastrophes played themselves out.

The lynx paused on a ridge, his belly tight, eyes spotting caribou at the bottom of the valley. The hare famine hurt, yet he survived well enough as long as caribou calves walked his country. The calves grew slowly. Each kill was a little more difficult than the last, but he had no capacity to foresee where this led.

The giant codfish sailed, belly distended with gargantuan eating of herring and crab, shellfish and lobster, carrion and cod, and he left a trail of vomited shells and carapaces cooked red by his powerful digestion. He sailed, majestic now in his bulk, in search of one last meal that would satisfy his hunger.

Heat sank into the body of the Gulf and into the plankton legions, and the petrel danced, carefree as a moth, in an ocean of food. The robin feasted in a forest now crawling with life, and the eagle, brought to earth again by the tireless salmon, flopped his gorged body clumsily away from a northern stream. The heat of the summer penetrated every pore of life, and the Gulf turned thankfully in its balm.

But the herring of the southern shallows were in the grip of a plague.

Plagues passed through the tissues of the Gulf in cycles. Plagues struck without the permission of the Gulf, yet powerful arguments could be made that they were necessary. A plague of fire seemed needed along the robin's western shore where the forests were decadent and slow-growing with age. Plagues were impartial; they destroyed seaweeds and attacked the lungs of ducks. The hares of the Gulf had some kind of plague, but its effects were insignificant. When plague invaded a big nation the Gulf paused in awe at the consequences.

178

A fungus, mystery-born in a purple night current, had reached the southern Gulf herring in the spring and had settled, patient and quiet, into their hearts and muscles. There it had worked toward consuming them. Unaware, they passed through the spring and early summer while the fungus matured and became lethal.

The infected fish swam weakly and lolled on their sides. The petrel saw their silver underbellies glistening as she sped away from her island toward the southern strait. The circling Gulf current took the herring slowly along the western shores of the big island and packed them, struggling feebly against death, into the wide bays and inlets there. Later, waves cast them ashore like stricken capelin at spawning time. In the heat the beaches reeked in a few days, and crows and ravens gathered and gulls clustered in hectic groups.

Many herring, feeling the fungus paralyzing them, dived. But they died underwater as certainly as those on the surface. Plankton bloomed without being grazed; copepods swarmed around dazed herring and were ignored. The dead and dying floated, fresh and glittering, green and petrified, rotting to disintegration. In a month, half of all the herring in the Gulf had died.

At the bottom the cod responded immediately. They swarmed in from offshore ledges and from deep water, darkening the bottom with their bodies. They ate the dying and the dead, and their feast started an immediate chain reaction. During plague they would feed almost without pause on herring flesh. By the fall most of them would have gained two or three pounds, weight that would be lost after the disappearance of the herring.

All territorial rules of lobster life were abrogated in favor of the herring feast. The lobsters gathered and ripped and tore at the piles of bodies and scuttled away with chunks of flesh in their claws. Each sought a place to bury his booty and then return to the feast. Meanwhile flounder waited vainly on the eastern fringes of the shallows, expecting the herring to spawn and provide them with *their* annual feast of herring eggs. But few fish spawned this year. The flounder might go hungry, but the gulls and murres and puffins feasted. They crisscrossed the ocean, and breeding cities almost everywhere in the Gulf prospered on tons of herring flesh.

The Gulf-shallows herring nation would not, however, be wiped out. Instead the odd few million survivors, those who lived through the summer, would recover from the plague and would be transformed by their survival. They would winter with difficulty, many of them depleted by the disease, but in the spring of the next year, as though imbued with a cosmic energy, they would begin spawning early and they would spawn throughout the spring and summer. They would spawn deep into fall until their exhausted bodies gave up and died, eggs and milt still oozing from them. By this act of frenzied procreation they would restore the lost population. They would set in motion a younger generation stronger than before, which carried within it a resistance to the plague.

The fungus, however, was not yet done. The waiting

flounder, rewarded at last by a few fish of the stricken generation, ate the eggs and were themselves stricken. They reeled away into deeper water and died. Alewives, passing across the shallows on their way east, picked up the fungus and carried it with them. They would carry it through the winter and bring it back into the Gulf the following year. They might migrate successfully upstream, but the fungus would be resurgent even as they tried to spawn; sick and dying, they would come tumbling down their rivers. A mackerel nation passing through the shallows caught the disease, matured it through the late summer, and was sent tumbling south with it in the fall, leaving a spoor of stricken fish behind as it fled.

Epidemics were weapons that struck the prosperous, destroying those creatures who had appealed to the Gulf for relaxation of the rules of balance. Epidemics were trials to test the corporate strength of nations, and their challenge reset the clocks of history.

II

Disease worked obscure changes in the tunnels of forests and in the shallows of dusky streams high in the mountains. Disease modified the life of the Gulf in a million different ways, yet rarely with visible effects. The robin saw another robin asleep on the branch of a tree and flew

181

to scold him out of his territory. But the interloper, head thrust into his fluffed-out back feathers, did not waken, nor would he waken. A virus worked in his lungs.

No creature of the Gulf was immune; no commonwealth ever had complete security from disease. It struck in any way it chose, picking out individuals, or families, or entire populations in a single valley, a gully in the sea, an island. It might annihilate or merely decimate, and then again it might not choose to kill at all.

Crowded along the southern and western shores of the mainland, the oysters of the southern Gulf were suffering from a disease as mysterious in its symptoms as it was uncertain in its strength. About half the oysters were affected and millions had died in this second year of the disease; many millions more were weakened under the stress. There was nothing dramatic about the sickness. It was a wasting away of tissue, and it made the oysters thin and weak before they died. Few recovered, but some remained fat and then died suddenly. Others developed yellowish-green pustules on their flesh.

This summer, with its heat, its slowing currents and clinging sea zephyrs, matured the disease. It moved steadily west along the southern Gulf, ranging forward about one mile a day in its progression from bay to bay, inlet to estuary, and left behind it ninety sick oysters out of every hundred. The summer gave the epidemic a sweep that cleaned out the southern Gulf, leaving a few staggered survivors. It swept up the western coast, annihilating populations as it went. Later it would cross to the big island

and obliterate the coastal oysters there. The process would take ten years, but the plague had leisure time to spare. At the end, when it came into the southern shallows again, it would find the southern oysters resurgent with the progeny of plague survivors and migrants from other nations—all immune, at least temporarily. Then, at the place of its genesis, the mysterious plague of the oysters would become extinct in the Gulf.

This oyster epidemic was not visible above the surface. Starfish, desperate at the disappearance of their food, turned to other shellfish, any shellfish, and destroyed many populations. The bottom feeders and many small fish, crabs, and lobsters fed on the diseased oysters and were not affected by the lethal organism. The sea plague was quiet, discreet, undramatic. It could not match the visible destruction of another epidemic on the mainland.

It was, perhaps, less a plague than a continuing attack on trees by insects which could become epidemic at the touch of the wind or the sun. The balsam fir—beautiful, robust balsam fir—was the first to be struck, victim of an army of tiny moths which had broken free from wintering chrysalids in the spring and had flown off through the forest to lay eggs. The eggs had hatched, releasing a flood of slender larvae which crawled over thousands of square miles of trees. In this summer they would defoliate entire forests. They would begin at treetops and not stop until they reached the lowest branches and the forest lay dead.

The white eagle, cruising the western fringe of the Gulf, saw a forest dying, but it meant nothing to him. The

183

lynx moved heedlessly through the infested forests, saw dry foliage gathering underfoot, and suspected nothing of the disaster overhead. If he survived his slaughter of the caribou and his frantic burrowing for mice, the death of this forest eventually would create the best hunting any lynx had ever known. The forest would fall, and among its twisted limbs a ravening horde of new trees and shrubs would grow. In this place a complete new world would be created for the hares of the future, and for the caribou. The epidemic in the treetops, now only a haunting, silent chaos, was the beginning of a strident future cosmos.

III

The epidemics raged on, and the Gulf felt the agony of them, measured by that reduction of tissue which permitted the re-creation of new life. The animals lived under the code of the Gulf, and so, eventually, did the plants. Midsummer, and the peak of epidemic passed, and it was now a time of drought, most evident along the western shore. Without rain the forest slowed and crackled, already decadent with fallen limbs and trunks and an overcrowding of shrubs and plants everywhere. It was a forest aching for tomorrow. Yet, despite the drought, nothing changed, no hopeful sight of smoke on any distant ridge, no gale to blow down these leaning trees. The heat mounted in hot blue skies and all clouds fled the Gulf. The big island, usually cool and mist-laden even in midsummer, felt the heat, and suffered in its thin soils.

In the Gulf the swordfish basked and dozed at the surface, the sturgeon wallowed in rapidly warming water. In the shallowest parts of the southern Gulf the water became tropically warm. The cod and haddock, cool-loving fish, touched this water and turned back, unable to stand such warmth.

The western shore suffered the heat most. Sheltered bays glittered and thrust out hard rods of reflected light. The heat concentrated without escape between the ridges of low mountains flanking valleys; it was held in these troughs of land. At the same time a movement of air from the southwest came steadily up the coast, which was nowhere relieved by the usual cool ocean breezes. The new air, dry and hot, poured over the intervening ranges and dropped into western valleys. The eagle sailed high as a cloud, felt the uprush of this new air, and allowed himself to be carried away. The heat in the forest was not his concern, yet he would be involved by its effect on the coastal rivers and inland tributaries. Already some of the fish in the streams, particularly those prowling the shallows, were suffering. Young salmon, gills working rapidly, clotted together and thrust their noses against tiny trickles of spring water coming into the mainstream. Suckers tried to avoid the heat by dropping to the deepest pools and hiding under roots deep in the shade.

After four days of steady, northward-moving air and

185

unbroken clear skies, the heat was unbearable. The clustering salmon became too thick; those that broke away from the spring trickles died and floated downstream. The heat reached into the deepest pools and drove out the suckers. They tried to escape in rapid, downstream swimming, but the water was too hot, and they died and joined the drifting salmon.

Soon the river system was uniformly hot. Rapids, waterfalls, natural weirs, even fast-running water offered no relief for the gasping fish. The alewives, hard hit in the tributaries of a large river, were wiped out in thirty-six hours, and their bodies, more than four million of them, rolled downriver to join the salmon and the suckers. The dead fish gathered in heaving, sinister eddies. The eagle soared no longer. He flew heavily from one point of disaster to another, and ate so well that at times he could not fly. Once, escaping from the sharp-swift attack of a wolf, he crashed into the center of a river and had to thrash ignominiously to shore. He saw bears stupefied with fish, sitting on hot beaches, mouths agape with the combination of heat and food.

The bodies drifted, the animals ate, the tributaries were cleared of fish. Shad, spawners in lower reaches of western rivers, were facing suffocation from heat at the farthest northern point of their range in the hemisphere, as far from the heat of the south as they could get. But the heat followed them. The eagle found the first of them on the seventh day of the heat buildup. Some of the shad were able to flee into the brackish water of the river estuaries;

186

others made it out to sea; but the standfasts died. Eventually, after the drought was broken, their rotting remains would be united with other victims from higher in the river: the alewives, the young salmon, the suckers, the trout.

The heat moved across the Gulf, as oppressive as ice, and sent the plankton scurrying and the herring dashing forward. Great swordfish, replete with mackerel, wallowed in enjoyment of the sun, their high dorsal fins and tails erect and rocking back and forth. Gulls shouted at them from high places in the hot sky.

IV

The heat affected all the creatures. Dripping with water, the robin emerged from the river shallows after his fifth bath of the day and a hawk watched him from a nearby tree, too tired to chase robins this day. The giant cod, feeling the heat in the Gulf, passed through the southern strait and found coolness below the big island where many layers of temperature offered him easy release from the Gulf heat. The lynx gasped at the heat and looked from a branch at the caribou whose hooves he must risk if he wanted to eat. Only the grilse, far to the east and in a thousand feet of black water, was unaffected by the drought.

187

The western end of the Gulf shallows was dominated by a colony of scallops which had been settled there for ten years. They were offspring of the main scallop nation beyond the southern strait, but nowhere near equaled the mothering stock in size. They had settled in the Gulf accidentally, after a twisting of currents during one frenzied spring of heavy gales had brought scallop eggs into the Gulf and dumped them at random. Those that had settled in the southern waters had survived. The local currents being favorable, they gradually extended their grip in the shallows. As they grew, starfish moved in around them and became dependent on scallop hunting, and the two creatures balanced each other's growth in mutual search for the limits of their new territory.

The drought remained static, the heat smothering. Then, surprisingly, a steady wind emerged from the east. It was neither blustery nor soft, neither cool nor hot. It was a benign, bloodless wind that promised nothing. It just blew, and blew, and blew. The eagle faced into it and hung motionless as a cloud. The lynx sniffed it suspiciously and smelled the countless odors of the offshore: the taint of rotting plankton killed in a collision of currents, the smell of iodine and salt and seaweed, the whiff of seabirds. There was something strange, nevertheless, about this wind. It gradually moved all the warm surface water off the southern shallows. It pulled this surface water solidly against the southwestern shores of the Gulf. It built up the water in bays and inlets, in rocky coves and along beaches until the pressure of the arriving water become insupportable.

The inshore water began to turn down, as though it were a withdrawing wave pulling itself back out to sea and hugging the bottom. The piled-up water responded to this release by flooding quickly back east, still deep underwater.

This was something more than the simple flight of shore-trapped seawater. It was the creation of a new current. Such was the pressure introduced by that constant, harmless wind from the east that the warm water swept the bottom on a broad front and headed for the northwest corner of the southern shallows. It reached the scallop nation three days later. The water-gulping shellfish felt the deadly warmth running through their bodies. Some clamped their shells shut, sensing that the change in temperature was dangerous. Others opened very wide, as if pleading for cool water. Some took flight and batted themselves frantically together in midwater before turning over, settling, and dropping to the bottom again.

The warm water flowed for days, slowed its pace, increased again, and then diminished. But the scallops, shocked, dazed, and dying, struggled on for a lunar cycle. Shells gaped, eyes dulled, and all filtering stopped. Crabs ducked in and out of the shells in a seasonal feast they would not soon see again. The giant cod, a cautious immigrant from deeper water, returned to the shallows in a flood of cool replacement water and fell among the stricken scallops. Now, instead of swallowing shellfish whole, he found he could insert his lips into the gaping shells and suck out the flesh. It was a treat and he enjoyed it, ignoring

189

the lobsters who scuttled around him in the scallop grave-yard.

The scallops would continue to die into the winter, and miles of open shells would twist and turn in the new winter currents. With all the shellfish dead, the starfish would be stricken, but the giant cod would not see them being bowled by currents along the bottom, bodies formed into hoops, searching blindly for new hunting grounds. He would be safe in deep water by that time, the hungry starfish beyond his ken or care.

Chapter TWELVE

I

The Gulf lay prostrated by heat. Its dry tissues crackled as marshes dried out and lakes diminished. The heat sent creatures into the earth to sleep away the drought and invited fire to invade the breathless forests. On some days the sun seemed strong enough to set the Gulf on fire spontaneously, but even the most decadent forests refused to burn. No ordinary fire would do now; it would need to be a conflagration.

The robin found refuge in the deep forest and hunted along the banks of streams which had shrunk in the drought but still possessed mud and damp earth flanks

191

where worms gathered. The eagle became a stream and river hunter. From the shade of red spruce he watched for unwary salmon desperate to find cooling springs and threw himself into the water, eating and bathing away the heat at the same time. In the big bird bazaars, particularly in the dense colonies of nesting murres, the heat was a killer. It spread stubby wings of nestlings, prostrated them, and roasted them alive. Around them, eggs exploded and the stench of rotting bodies and putrid eggs clogged the nostrils of the surviving colony dwellers. In the gull colonies young gulls deserted their nesting territories and huddled together under trees or in the shade of rocks. They collected along rock shorelines and bathed vigorously. Only the petrel, in her deep and cool burrow and with her long, nocturnal flights to and from the island, felt little of the heat.

A small thundercloud appeared out of nowhere and grew quickly. It settled in foothills behind the western shore and stood there, bristling with suppressed activity, before it lanced down one spare finger of fire. The timing was perfect, and with the job done, the cloud dispersed. The hills became clear and hot again, and the shore continued to receive the endless warm water of the rivers flowing out to it.

The thundercloud disappeared, but as if summoned on cue the east wind, which had been quiescent for days, took up its complementary work. It riffled the shore and probed among the forest trees. Somewhere in the forest the second stage of the thundercloud's work began. The forefinger of flame had landed in the clumpy head of a balsam fir, broken twenty years before and double-branched from its leader. It was loaded with dead and dying tissue from the insect attack. It ignited in a second, blazed like a torch for minutes, then dwindled to a thick-smoked smolder.

The wind arrived, its timing tardy but not too late, and struck the balsam fir. The tree glowed and the smoke streamed away. In the next second a tongue of flame leaped out. A touch, a caress of wind, and the fire jumped.

It jumped, and touched the next tree and that tree exploded in a red column. The fire vaulted inland and ran at sixty miles an hour. A ghastly roaring, a series of thunderclaps, explosions, hissing side excursions, and the fire was gone with the burned and burning in its wake. As an afterthought, the fire left behind some sober flames to consume what its headlong, erratic advance had not destroyed. These flames burned thoroughly and systematically, razing everything which had been spared by that first flush of flame.

The robin, standing atop a tall fir in the heat, saw the black-and-white cloud gushing upward to the northeast, but it meant nothing to him, and he fell, wings limp, back into the shade.

The Gulf wind which had energized the fire stopped; the vanguard of flame reached the peaked ridge of the first inshore mountains. The wind expired and the fire smoke plumed upright, then turned uncertainly as it responded to slow southern air coming up the farther slope of the

the ridge. It meandered along the ridge, moving southeast now. In places it ran back on itself and so completed the damage it had done in its first foray. An enormous long gray cloud moved out into the Gulf. It gently smothered the petrel's island and she smelled the smoke, an alarming smell, with her nestling warm under her chest and nowhere near ready to fly. The gray cloud swept east, over the southern shallows, and died eventually in a hard blue sky.

Now split a hundred ways, the fire advanced on a twenty-mile front back toward the Gulf. It thrust arms of flame up nearby valleys. It encircled and destroyed. It remained stationary for a time and burned everything to a black crisp. The robin vaulted to the tip of a fir at the smell of smoke. To every woodland creature smoke was a signal that needed no previous experience to understand. He saw the smoke now well spread. To the north it ran west into the Gulf. To the south it rose very high and menacing, and to the west mountains were shrouded in it. His impulse was flight, but the signal was not yet that imperative. He had no stimulus to fly one way or another.

A small thundercloud, perhaps a reincarnation, appeared in the hills of the big island. Darkly menacing, it rippled with suppressed energy. The crackling spruces cried out for water, and the cloud sent it down. But in the hot air the water dissolved into vapor again and the dark cloud dropped a crooked finger and blasted a trembling aspen to the ground. The tree lay dead and smouldering. The lynx started up in his den. He smelled the smoke of the explosion and ran to the entrance. He saw the thunder-cloud twist with fire; the sky growled and the cloud fled down the valley.

In a moment the big island was on fire.

The fires burned around the Gulf in a valedictory statement for much of the forest. They reached the southern shore in two pockets, hissed, and swept the debris of centuries into molten rubbish. Behind, they left a remnant of pain and countless wreaths of thin, tired smoke. On the western shore the fire struck the defenseless birches, which died to a tree. It raced through the dense balsam fir forests and wiped them out. Havoc followed the fire's work among the hardwoods. Their leaves blackened and shriveled and burned and were whisked away before the long-lasting fires of their tough trunks began.

The robin watched the smoke gathering above him, heard the crackle of flames in the distance, and then, without further hesitation, fled downstream toward the Gulf.

The fires burned with intensive variations from region to region. Along the banks of rivers they accepted the support of winds bleeding from the continental interior and burned downstream so fast they killed nothing but raced at treetop level and sucked out the air from among the trees. In places they pulled up unwilling birds and moths and flies and bees. In the valley of the lynx the fire burned with deliberation; it burned from the tops of trees down, burned the trunks, and then went into the roots. Given the chance, it burned the ground, consuming fertility that had built up over thousands of years. Behind, it left scorched

195

rock and the smoking skeletons of incinerated victims. The lynx turned back at the ridge to look at his valley, but he could see nothing. Dense smoke lay between the valley ridges and the thick smoke rolled downhill like viscid water toward the sea. He saw another lynx, his mate, disappear down the slope behind him and after a sigh, he followed her.

II

The fire burned on. Along the western shore its fuel was three hundred years dry, and burned to nothing. But the creatures of the fire were young and most urgently anxious not to join the conflagration. The refugees passed silently through the canopy or above it; warblers and thrushes, vireos, sapsuckers, robins, sparrows, bluebirds, orioles all united in this oddest of migrations.

The grackles, who ignored everybody except fellow blackbirds, found themselves flying with robins and bluebirds and even warblers, whom they would have eaten in different times. The escape flight testified to the power of wings, to the marvelous freedom they provided, but said nothing about the nests and nestlings and half-flighted youngsters left behind. Millions of them faced the red mask of the approaching flame alone.

The nests of the orioles burned well, flamed incandescent for a second as the early fire caught them, and the soundless victims inside died without even seeing their killer. Nest holes full of young flickers droning their disapproval of the smoke and heat became roasting hot, and the droning choked among the sound of falling branches. By the shores of a river, wood ducklings leaped and fell but ran into the forest and suffocated before they burned. A branch lined with chickadees exploded in bright puffs of golden flame.

The half-fledged birds knew the danger, knew to turn away from the fire, and they flew, short tails flared in panic, necks arched foward, as they attempted to reject the upmoving ground. Down to earth they fell among underbrush; then flew again, but not so far this time; and flew again a short distance, and then ran, pathetic in a forest dominated by the roar of flames.

The refugee insects faced the flames. They could fly, but few escaped. Spiders spun trailing lines of silk and used the heat of the fire to waft them up and away, thousands of vaulting feet into the air. Some even flew over the Gulf on their threads, although millions spun away to death in the water where herring or ctenophores and other creatures of the plankton ate them. But most of the insects stood fast and died. The sawflies and horntails, once omnipotent forest destroyers, spread their dainty double wings and arched their yellow-ringed bodies, and died in midair, crisped in flame. Praying mantises reared up in astonishment at the wall of flames fronting them, and exploded in flashes of yellow fire.

197

Tiger beetles ran, desperate with the heat scorching their backs, and died as they had lived—black, but smoking now. The wasps flew and seemed safe, but their notion of refuge was a place under a leaf or concealment inside a nest, and their tree nests exploded in futile bursts of flame while the leaves curled and fled. Dragonflies and butterflies, and webworms, budworms and moths, leaf rollers and cankerworms, and billions and billions of caterpillars twisted and turned in the heat, flipped and fell into the holocaust.

All the work of this summer in the forest was made null as the robber flies fled with the horseflies, and tent caterpillar shelters were whipped off the crotches of trees, leaving the caterpillars in midair for a second before falling.

The refugees poured away in flight from the fire all around the Gulf. The lynx, who had started his flight from the fire in leisurely fashion, uncertain whether he should leave his familiar valley, was now running like everybody else. The wind had risen, had taken the flames out of the valley, and the sound of them seemed closer every moment. The woods around him filled with smoke and the querulous cries of confused and frightened songbirds. He saw three wolves drift through the trees ahead of him, heard the rumble of caribou feet, and saw mice moving underfoot although they lacked much knowledge of the world's extent and were not really going anywhere.

At the southern-shore fire, raccoons and skunks stepped out into the dreaded daylight and moved away from the flames. Rabbits and deer joined them, ignoring, for the moment, a cougar sniffing into the wind at the approaching smoke. The smoke rose over the Gulf and the flames rumbled on many horizons, and everywhere teeming mice and lemmings and voles and shrews of the forest floor bounded from their burrows and nests and made short, stabbing runs. But they quickly sought cover, and burrowed deeper, and were later overtaken by the fire and died already interred.

The fires burned on for weeks, and when they were done, so was the summer. The two conclusions coincided as precisely as if planned. The Gulf lay exhausted—burned, brown, black, smoking, its tissues desiccated by the pull of the drought and the draw of the fires. The robin, driven out into the Gulf by the flames and the heat around him, had panicked and turned north, mistakenly assuming he was turning toward land. He realized his mistake almost too late when the sun emerged through the thick pall of the fires. He turned back and reached the southern coast exhausted.

The forest birds flew cautiously along the fringes of the burns, their territories destroyed or rendered unrecognizable and the meaning of their northern summer made senseless. The eagle, hovering very high, witness to the extent of the fires, saw burned land stretching out of sight, but he had no way to make order of such destruction either, so he wheeled back to his northern shore patrol.

III

The fires done, rains falling, the autumn a breath away, the Gulf had to face the reconstruction, the regeneration of its body. The work began immediately. Unimaginable numbers of tree seeds were already in the wind, parachute-borne, traveling fine as dust, aloft in the company of spores, stuck to the feet of birds or lodged in their crops. Some seeds came into the burns from the northern shore, some from distant continental valleys, others from the south. The seeds cooperated with each other; the big island was as likely to provide seeds for the southern shore as that shore was to send its seeds north across the Gulf.

The richest area of the Gulf was the western shore and regeneration began there, not only because of its earth wealth but because it had been the most desperately needful of revolutionary change. The dead red spruces, like tall black fingers in the expiring sun, beckoned the seeds of poplar and birch which drifted in like smoke. The poplar seeds, lightest of all, came thickest because they had gathered in the air from the most distant parts. They were fast to sprout, fast to grow, and fast to discourage other trees. It would be many years before the red spruce could displace these interlopers and re-create the forest that had been destroyed.

200

On high ground along valley ridges and hills where the fires had been most destructive, balsam fir would create a single-tree forest by the sheer density of its invasion of the burn. Millions of seedlings would sprout, thick enough to mat the ground at the first touch of rain. Fast growers, they would thin themselves in a few years to about a hundred thousand stems to the acre, all the while fighting for a share of moisture and space, air and sunlight, and killing each other as ruthlessly as fire. Finally, about six thousand trees would survive and grow to maturity on every acre burned that disastrous summer.

The fire, however, had not carried all before it. While it had appeared to destroy in some places, it had been tricked by the trees whose habits had been changed by other fires. When the fire hit the black spruce, that tough colonizer of thin soils and soggy pits and bogs, that survivor for five thousand uninterrupted years, it did not kill. Rather, it created. The black spruce had anticipated this fire. The cones at the top of their stems had accumulated for years without opening like those lower on the trees. Came the fire; the heat struck; the cones, seeds unharmed, opened after the fire had gone, and the seeds fluttered down, first to recolonize the burn.

The jackpine forests which had smothered the river lowlands along the western shore also welcomed the fire. Their branches reached out for the flames and drew them toward their cones. Obediently the cones responded to the heat of the fire and yawned open after it had passed, and a smothering host of seeds waited for the rains.

201

IV

The fires had come and gone. Externally they seemed one summer's rebuff to the Gulf, but internally they were part of an immensely slow and ancient process by which the Gulf was shaped. On the big island a solitary fire had started on the parched east coast, far from the lynx's territory, and had run a hundred miles before being knocked out by a thick mist boiling up from the east. Neither the trees nor the land were ready for this fire. They had colonized the thin acid soil with difficulty and a patience that had anticipated an abundance of time. Thick mists had quenched any hint of fire on that coast for several thousand years; no other Gulf forest could claim kinship with this old and sacred place. It was even older than it seemed. Concealed inside the forest that existed before the fire were the remains of an earlier forest. Giant logs lay partially buried in bogs; the stumps of huge trees protruded from mounds of moss. This older forest had reached up the coast, riding from valley to hilltop, marching down mountain ranges and pushing as far north as possible under the benign winds of a five-thousand-year-long period of warmth. Abruptly, the benevolence vanished; the arctic winds blew down. The forest froze in a sarcophagus of its own construction.

202

But another forest came back, its trees not as big as the limits of the old forest and solidly emplaced. Fir and spruce thrived and, miraculously, many valley stands of white pine, groaning at the winter cold. In the territory of this forest lay a holdover from the extinct one which had transformed the even sweep of purple hills and pallid lakes and rock-boned mountains into a tick in the time clock of the big island. Thousands of tiny hollows in peat bogs studded the eastern shore. Debris and soil had collected in these pockets from the ice age, and there a tiny fern grew. It was of no account by the measurement of great whales and codfish herds and the sweep of balsam fir staining distant hills, but it had survived in the pockets, sheltered from the winter wind by a lip of shielding soil, plants, leaves, and rocks. It was not more than an inch or two high.

It was there, huddled down after waiting in invisible spores for most of the year. It had waited through thousands of tumultuous winter winds which had killed the old forest and pushed all the new forest trees back from the coast and deformed them in sheltered places. It waited as snowstorms buried the island in violent aftermath of the warm period. It waited until the end of summer each year when it released its spores to the wind and disappeared back into the earth.

The forests had conquered the big island in phalanxes pushing northward. But the fern was a loner. Its nearest kind was a thousand miles to the south. It was demonstrably a warm-climate plant, and its presence on the big

203

island a puzzle. Had it somehow survived the ice age with its spores quiescent for thousands of years in the frozen muck of the island? Had it lain there for millennia while the glaciers ground the earth? Or had it reached the island along some extraordinary highway which consisted entirely of peat bogs, certain kinds of soil, and tiny potholes for the fern's refuge, a highway unbroken from the south to this remote north, no trace of which remained?

The plume of smoke had swirled and spread and the fire had come up the coast. It had advanced in some places underground and burned the humus soil first, so that the living trees collapsed into a burning midden of ancient matter and were consumed. It burned every trace of the older forest. It incinerated the petrified trunks and atomized the moss. The tiny ferns strained to release their spores before it was too late, but too late it was, and their long northern adventure was ended. The forest fell, and was gone, and the refugee birds would not return to this place for a thousand generations, and a forest might never grow here again.

Chapter THIRTEEN

I

Fall, and the skies swirled gray and old-man clouds fled west while the east wind ransacked the beaches and coves of the Gulf for a trace of summer. The burned land, its scorched smell washed away, glowed pale green while the black trunks of fire victims were still falling. It was autumn, and time for retreat. The Gulf was tired of the old season and its creatures must be gone, sent to safer places for the oncoming winter. The giant cod felt the change earlier than his comrades and drifted offshore, away from the dangerous land. Snow fell tentatively on the highlands of the big island. The lynx's feet, broadening in readiness for winter, scrunched among the trees. Caribou clustered in this new valley. They looked up at him. A hare, coat blotched halfway toward all white, fled downhill, a hint that the hunger was over. The eagle, with pungent memories of this season, paused over the northern strait and looked down and saw thin lines of migrants moving from the arctic.

The sight of the migrants made him restless, an unwilling witness. His failed summer haunted him. He allowed himself to drift east across the gray strait to the big island. He turned for the Gulf shore, majestically at ease on the wing, and floated inland. The land rose steadily in a series of terraces toward the inland mountains where, many years before, he had hunted and bred on a crag overlooking a steep-sided valley. He looked now for the familiar place but the forest had burned and nothing was recognizable. He drifted on south.

Mountains rolled down into lowland country, and crowberries and partridgeberries and whortleberries drew migrant birds. The eagle watched tiny forms speeding down valleys and across the barrens and heard the faint, hollow cries. He flew across the north-south tracks of caribou, saw wolves sunning themselves on rocks and bears prowling the edge of a river. A lynx, running sharp as the edge of a leaf, disappeared in joyful pursuit of the white-blotched hare.

Catching an updraft, the eagle rose, and in time the southern strait came into view. From an immense height he saw the mighty Gulf paling into green infinity, felt it dying, withdrawing from him, diminishing his hold on this place, and he was lost. He looked into the interior of the big island, row upon row of purple hills stretching inland, intersected by chromium lakes, and the whole of it held so achingly still that it, too, must be dying.

He turned west, crossed the strait, curved south, and flew for a day along the southern coast, flew due west, flew into the late-summer burns, and into the interior, and in this way, this individual eagle, this white eagle, left the Gulf.

II

Before the fall could mature the Gulf must be emptied of its harvest of seabirds. The petrel, a faithful servant to her single nestling for nearly fifty days, stopped feeding him one night. She returned to the island, circled, and cried out, but did not enter her burrow. Her youngster heard the cries, recognized them among the thousands of others, and waited. But no shuffling sounded at the entrance. In the early morning the petrel flew out to sea and criss-crossed the Gulf waters until dawn. Restless, she felt the pull of the island and the tug of the sea. She had fed her youngster fat; she had made him heavier than she was, plump for his departure. But now, alone in that dusky burrow, he was gone from her forever. She could not aid his departure. She could not fly with him through the surrounding spruces. She could not guide him in darkness from the island. She had abandoned him. In daylight she passed through the southern strait and out of the Gulf for the last time this year.

In the great puffin cities along the Gulf's northern shore and around the coasts of the big island, the adult puffins streamed away from their young, fled the Gulf completely. They flew in compact groups down the western coast of the island. They poured steadily through the southern strait in the wake of the petrel. Some pushed through the northern strait, joining the arctic drift, and came south with it. They were all bound for appointments on the open sea where they would molt and face the winter more warmly clad.

Behind them, deserted puffin nestlings waited in their burrows and, like the petrel, consumed their body fat until the moment when hunger would drive them out to meet the open sea.

In the gannetries the bond between parent and nestling had already withered away. The youngsters, fat as the other young seabirds, gathered together in groups. They ignored their parents and were ignored by them, as though all understood that the fall offered independence to both groups. For those young gannets on the tops of tall cliffs, the first flight meant a fall into the abyss, and they looked down doubtfully at the distant gray water.

Depart. Leave the Gulf. The message was pervasive and spread over many days through mixtures of changing winds, rains, mists. The murres gathered on low islands in a growing uproar of voices. Nestlings and adults mixed together, all animated by the message of the fall, which invited them into the sea. At dusk armies of them marched resolutely forward, breasted the water, and then swam and bathed and dived in delight at being free from the tyranny of the land. Young murres, grown on cliffs, jumped to infinity, flanked closely by adults until they crashed into the sea.

Resolute, the young gannets jumped too, and some flew well enough to flutter into distant collisions with the sides of waves. Others crashed into rocks and bounced on their own body fat into the freedom of the water. Now fasted slender, the young puffins came to the entrances of their burrows, looked out, saw the sea, and ran, then flew awkwardly toward it. The young petrel, also well fasted, came out of his burrow at midnight, flopped on the ground through the spruces, kicked himself into the air, and arrowed into the black fastness of the sea night.

The gull colonies exploded and dispersed their members in every direction. Youngsters and adults alike waited at the threshold of the migration route and picked out the shorebirds as they landed, exhausted from arctic flights. They waited at dawn on a hundred islands for tardy youngsters making their first flights toward the sea. Some tested the temper of the Gulf to see whether they could winter in it. Others flew into the center of the continent or drifted south with the migrants, and some made a long migration into the subtropics.

209

Young kittiwakes fell from their lofty cliffs and felt none of the southern impulse. They had no communication with the hastening throngs passing south. Instead they moved with perfect aplomb out to sea, moved east in flights that would take some of them halfway around the earth across the open water.

III

The Gulf in the fall had its messengers, representatives who slid into it from the north. Shorebirds on hemispheric missions brought with them quick, passing reminders that the arctic lay over the Gulf and could return any time it wished. The shorebirds came south from mist-shrouded beaches and solitary black islands, from the tundra and its summer ponds, from a successful assault against the northernmost capacity of the earth to accept them. The Gulf was a staging area where they paused to gather breath, to consider, to fatten, and to prepare for great leaps into the south. They arrived breathless and haunted coastlines like scraps of motion only half seen as they settled into quiet inlets and smothered mudbanks or stood reflected in glassy-smooth pools.

The shorebird migration into the Gulf did not resemble the urgent thrust of their northern spring. This was no drive to a place, no rush to fruition. It was, rather,

210

a reluctant, almost leisurely retreat with many backward glances at the ice and snow touching the deserted tundra country where they had bred. Some lingered as long as they dared and watched the gray clouds muffling flat horizons all around them. They heard the moan of hostile winds and remembered, as they grew hungry, the Gulf's crops of berries, the Gulf's sand and mud shorelines teeming with worms and eggs and larvae.

They set out in a confused mixture of intentions. They collected along the shores of an arctic sea and dozed in a chill east wind. In the morning many of them were gone, plucked cleanly from the ranks of their colleagues as they responded to directions as old as the land itself. They came south to the Gulf in groups best fitted to succeed in migration. Females flew together; males and youngsters, flying wing to wing, came by another route, a thousand miles behind the females. Their southern movement was thrust east, then west, by angry winds, and their arrival at any place was always in doubt.

The sandpipers gathered very early, while the Gulf was still in midsummer, before the fires had begun, and started a leisurely drift south. They walked quick-footed along beaches, then flew over the gray arms of the northern sea. They indulged themselves in quick northern flights as though changing their minds in mid-migration. Finally they reached the Gulf before the first flush of fall was evident, while the fires were still burning and the Gulf creatures were unaware that the season had changed around them. The sandpipers ran brightly at the edge of

211

crisp, advancing waves, followed in the flat, rushing with-drawal of water, and made the shoreline their own.

They collected in an estuary and settled so firmly into the tidal flats that they looked resident. They flew back and forth at dawn and dusk, from hunting territory to sleeping ground, and their great dense flocks roared down the strand. They turned back and forth to confuse the eyes of shore watchers, their gray backs showing solid, then changing quickly to white bellies, the flock thinning as it turned away and streamlined itself against the setting sun.

Around them, gray-washed, long-billed dowitchers waited, the females having arrived first at the Gulf and tested it with their long bills jabbed deep into estuarine mud, knowing the males would follow, knowing their nestlings were safely escorted.

The shore migrants spread themselves thin and in-consequential, but they came down steadily for ninety days, an uninterrupted flight in systematic desertion of the north. Sanderlings tarried along the western shore and were joined by first-year birds whose arrival pushed the adults farther south. The yellowlegs came down in a gentle flood, dropped into innumerable small seashore lakes and brackish pools, spread out across the thin line at the head of the tide, collected and waited the next call south. The plovers settled on clear, damp inshore ground on the southern shore, poking for worms and grubs in the grass.

Down came the shorebirds in their variegated thou-sands: the dowitchers and turnstones and snipe, and the phalaropes gathering in floating carpets along the southern

Gulf. Down they came: willets and whimbrels, curlews and knots, stilt sandpipers and avocets; the thread of birds continued from glacier to Gulf, from tundra to the edge of the ocean.

On the highlands of the eastern peninsula and along the southern fringe of the big island where berry crops awaited them, the curlews settled and fattened, knowing that when they jumped clear of the land this time they would fly direct into open sea and not stop until this fat berry flesh was gone and another shoreline lay under them.

They waited, tense and expectant, for a signal from the Gulf. It came just after dark sullen clouds collected in the west. The curlews' cries of melancholy invoked dead comrades who had made the northern flight possible and petitioned the Gulf for safe passage as they took off, leaving the beaches and barrens empty. In their wake a wind reached out for them, but found only footprints pointing south.

The constellation of shorebirds swelled, diminished, became an uproar of wings quickly gone, to be followed by new creatures fast behind. Golden plovers gathered on an island headland, keen-eyed and eager, all of them adults. Their nestlings were flying south on the route that had brought their parents north. Abruptly, the plovers were gone out to sea by a different route.

The shorebirds called out to the Gulf in voices that lingered—*kew-kew-kew*—calls sent into the vacuum of empty blue inlets, calls cut off in midsentence and left hanging interrogatively. Here, a smooth lake, silent, then

213

gray wings beating, one cry—*alloo!*—and the birds gone. Herringbone patterns on beaches, walking everywhere and nowhere, the footprint makers gone, perhaps dead, and the footprints obliterated in rising water.

The Gulf hastened the shorebirds along, and when they were gone nothing filled the void made by their departure.

IV

Retreat. Leave the Gulf. The message seemed clear. In the late summer the survivors of the earlier alewife carnage had made their run for the sea, fewer than one in ten surviving the moment of hatching. But their numbers were still great, and they escaped into the Gulf, running a gantlet of night herons. Once in the estuaries, they took canopies of terns and herring gulls into the Gulf with them.

Retreat. But not all life fled the Gulf. Some creatures were poised to assault the Gulf's western gates. The year was just beginning for them. The last run of salmon, united for a moment in the sea with the fleeing alewives, waited under the smoke of the fires and then, with the first fall rains, ran inland. Magnificent creatures these, all red flesh and full of fat, superb health built from leisurely feeding, scale colors shimmering with energy. They jumped;

214

they flew in a special brilliant spawning show for the Gulf.

But the spawning was difficult. The higher the salmon reached inland, the more cloudy the water. Heavy rains obscured their spawning redds with silt, an echo of the fire. With the dense pack of trees gone, the rain scoured earth from around numb roots of the dead and dying trees.

The salmon breathed silt, retreated choking, and advanced again, and the Gulf earth struggled to resist its loss of trees. The salmon swam by great raspberry groves, collections of still-tiny plants but destined to grow eight feet high in immediate response to the fire. The Gulf needed the fastest, thickest growth to save the salmon and its own soil. The raspberry fire crop would dominate burned earth for years while new trees struggled under them. Then, when the trees triumphed, the raspberries would concede their success and grow smaller until, ten years later, they would be back to their original positions and sizes in the forest.

Revolution or routine, all Gulf paths moved with life on journeys long or short. The caribou moved steadily down mountain trails toward the southern lowlands. The shrimp legions, the summer krill that fed the whales, left the Gulf's surface waters. Their juvenile lives at the surface were over, and they would now live permanently in the depths. They fell, every one of them a male, and headed toward molting and growing and copulating with females in the depths, and growing larger, and copulating again. And then, one winter, they would lose their testes and their sexual parts would be transformed into ovarian

215

tissue. By their fourth winter they would be females and copulate with the smaller, fallen males in the ingenious submarine Gulf.

The southern shallows chilled; the great oyster nation there faced its first threat of winter. Those who were infected with the boring sponges in their shells and had been busy all summer plugging the bore holes were caught in an odd dilemma. Unable to plug the holes as their bodies grew quiescent in response to chilling water, they continued to suffer helplessly the sponges who did not chill as early. The comatose oysters had one small weapon: clusters of blood cells would be mobilized on their flesh against the holes—the first step in repair to be completed, perhaps, in the spring. But oysters who had been badly attacked had already lost the fight and would die in the spring from attrition.

Cold air rolled down valleys, and horizons grayed. Eider ducks moved inshore toward meetings with ice which would soon cling to the coast. Scoters dived for mussels clustered along shorelines. The leaves rushed last colors into the Gulf, and the skies hastened with ancient, tired clouds.

Retreat. The brook trout followed the salmon in beginning their year. They had spent days working upstream, basking in fitful bright sun, unaffected by bursts of snow in high country or by heavy rains. They moved steadily on as the forests emptied and the northern refugees moved in to refill them. Some of the trout would not reach their breeding places until the end of the year. Then, in bitter

216

cold, they would scoop out their redds at the headquarters of streams and lay their eggs.

Even later were the tomcod. The main body prepared to ascend the longest western river, with hundreds of miles yet to travel before they spawned deep inland. By that time the new year would be well begun, and their adhesive eggs, stuck to the bottom of a shallowing river, would grow under ice.

V

Swordfish, nourished and rejuvenated by the Gulf, moved like fat sea pigs through the southern strait carrying a cargo of new flesh on their bones. Millions of smelts moved into estuaries all along the western shore, where they would stay until spring for early upriver spawning expeditions. Other migrants—sharks and dogfish, tarpons and dolphins, tuna and sailfish—left the Gulf in individual and collective travel, and their flight emptied the Gulf of some of the herring's worst enemies.

All creatures seemed to move even if they did not migrate to other climates. The great cod legions who had come into shallow coastal waters to feed during the summer tasted the change of season in water moved by autumnal gales. They followed the giant cod offshore. He, wiser than they, had threaded his way through a maze of

217

changing temperatures and flavors to find a winter refuge in deep, warm water.

Throughout the Gulf fish were moving vertically and horizontally in anticipation of the cold. The herring, fat by late summer, fell into congregations where they would spend the winter partially comatose and feeding on their fat. The haddock moved steadily over the southern fringes of the sunken sea plateau to winter places on the edges of the slopes.

The squid, finally surfeited with their summer slaughter at the big island, hastened south. They swept the southern strait clear of life, sank into deeper water as they felt the edge of a plateau approaching, and disappeared into the deepest, blackest waters of the ocean. Somewhere, far distant from the Gulf, they would spawn and create another squid invasion army for the following spring.

Along almost every Gulf shoreline the flounder retreated into deeper water, anonymously gray on gray sand, dark marks melting, and disappeared into winter gloom. And from the treacherous surface came a rain of creatures and eggs, all responding to the fall gales and an inborn knowledge that there was a place to survive the winter.

VI

After the fires the southern shore of the Gulf gathered in its cargo of songbirds, refugees from the wasted forests of east and west. The robin had reached there exhausted from his misguided Gulf flight and had fallen into the company of thousands of comrades. Responding universally to the flush of red and to the scatter of leaves, they dashed through the forest. A robin could expend the last of his life force at the Gulf and die there now, replete; and some did.

The robin felt the excitement; he shrieked and laughed and puffed out his russet breast and faced each dawn with joy.

As he waited, the songbirds of the Gulf disappeared. A plaintive whisper of a sparrow this day; tomorrow, silence. No spring flooding of creatures into new territory, this, but rather a whimper of departure. Pipits filled the air one afternoon and settled along a shoreline, then went out to sea by the tens of thousands. The rusty blackbirds had left the southern Gulf, and the fox sparrows, scratching in highland snow, would soon be gone. The songbirds simply faded away; vireos and flycatchers, warblers and sparrows drifted in inconspicuous assembly, a twitter in the dark, wingbeats in the rain.

Still the robin hesitated, his unwillingness to leave the Gulf shared by many others of his kind. Some, on the big island, turned and flew north again, back into the interior of the island, where they found blueberries and mountain ash and where they would remain until the real freeze began.

One morning the robin saw the Gulf gather itself into a gray, wet cloud and roll toward the shore. The weak sun went out. He turned south. He flew free, divorced from his progeny, his mate already dead. He flew jerkily, quick spasms of movement that united him with comrades, then sent him flying alone as he responded to the mysterious urgings and promptings of ancient memories. The robin knew where he was going, had a clear image of his destination, and flew at night well above the silent forest until he was a hundred miles south of the Gulf.

The robin remembered his destination, but he had no memory of his southern pathway. The entire continent waited to receive him and the southland of his winter territory was impatient for his arrival. Ahead, unexpected, one high tree on one high ridge; the robin fell in a tangle of nocturnal limbs.

VII

The shores of the Gulf flushed red as blood, paled into yellow indecision, the shades of color a blur of passing tints as shorebird and songbird rushed past. The colors washed into the waters of ponds and estuaries, were caught and held in upland lakes, were broken by young fish leaving the mountains to early-winter meetings in the sea. The colors suggested danger, and then maturity, and, finally, unconcern as the trees went to sleep. Here and there shorebirds became enraged by the colors and danced obscurely, ringing stricken comrades and menacing them with their beaks.

The water changed color as the plants and animals fell, leaving behind gray wastelands in which a herring might swim hungry for thirty days and where the petrel, if she were not already far distant in midocean, would not deign to pause.

The year was done, and every living thing in the Gulf was changed by it; yet the sense of the Gulf had not changed. It remained the anvil on which all other lives were forged. No amount of futile robins could alter its rhythm, and starving lynx or stricken herring were scarcely pinpricks on its bountiful surface. It ruled these lives with detached wisdom, though the desperate lynx had not seen this detachment; the malevolence would have killed him if he had not fought the Gulf. The giant cod's great rush for food had not been in waters of detachment; his hunting places were designed to test his need. The grilse had won his battle with the Gulf and would return, but he had found involvement, not detachment. Lives touched lives and were mutually affected, no part of the main separate, yet every life as individual as though created with no other life in mind.

With one last blush, the sun went down, and the snow replaced it. Far north, the seals heaved themselves up on their great arctic ice train. With so long to wait for their return, the Gulf closed its eye in sleep.